The Era of Not Quite

Winner, 2011 BOA Short Fiction Prize

THE ERA OF NOT QUITE

STORIES BY DOUGLAS WATSON

AMERICAN READER SERIES, NO. 19

BOA EDITIONS, LTD. ✦ ROCHESTER, NY ✦ 2013

For information about permission to reuse any material from this book please contact The Permissions Company at www.permissionscompany.com or e-mail permdude@eclipse.net.

Publications by BOA Editions, Ltd.—a not-for-profit corporation under section 501 (c) (3) of the United States Internal Revenue Code—are made possible with funds from a variety of sources, including public funds from the New York State Council on the Arts, a state agency; the Literature Program of the National Endowment for the Arts; the County of Monroe, NY; the Lannan Foundation for support of the Lannan Translations Selection Series; the Mary S. Mulligan Charitable Trust; the Rochester Area Community Foundation; the Arts & Cultural Council for Greater Rochester; the Steeple-Jack Fund; the Ames-Amzalak Memorial Trust in memory of Henry Ames, Semon Amzalak and Dan Amzalak; and contributions from many individuals nationwide. See Colophon on page 148 for special individual acknowledgments.

ART WORKS.
arts.gov

State of the Arts

NYSCA

Cover Design: Sandy Knight
Cover Photo: Elysia A. Smith
Cover Art: Dirty Bandits (Hand-painted Sign)
Interior Design and Composition: Richard Foerster

BOA Logo: Mirko

Library of Congress Cataloging-in-Publication Data

Watson, Douglas E., 1971–
[Short stories]
THE ERA OF NOT QUITE : stories / by Douglas Watson. — First edition.
    pages cm
Winner of the first annual BOA Short Fiction Prize.
ISBN 978-1-938160-10-3 (Paper) — ISBN (invalid) 978-1-938160-11-0 (E-book)
1. Short stories, American. I. Title.
PS3623.A86968E73 2013
813'.6—dc23

2012044330

BOA Editions, Ltd.
250 North Goodman Street, Suite 306
Rochester, NY 14607
www.boaeditions.org
A. Poulin, Jr., Founder (1938–1996)

In memory of
Coral Lee Watson

Contents

Against Specificity

The trouble: You want Thing A but are stuck with Thing B.

Shit, you say, turning Thing B around in your hands. Look at this thing, you say. It's as dull as a bucket of dirt. It's not half as interesting as a sculpture of a dog pissing on a dead man's shoe in the rain, and you don't have one of those. You don't have Thing A, either.

Hell, you haven't even seen Thing A. You've only heard about it from your neighbor, who works down at the Thing Exchange. What he or she said: Thing A shines like a gold tooth in the mouth of Jesus. Thing A is rounder, fuller, faster, zestier than Thing B. Thing A is perfect—it's what you need. Why, it even smells good, like waffles.

Your neighbor is a very reliable describer of things. For instance, he or she once described life as *the long slide into the box.* You've been thinking about this lately. The box doesn't bother you—it might even be cozy in there—but the lid freaks you way the heck out. Not much room, once that lid is in place. You've been sliding a long time now; better hurry up and get Thing A while you can still enjoy it.

On your way to the Thing Exchange, Thing B tucked under your arm, you run into someone—an unemployed magistrate, say, or a circus clown who comes up to you and says, I have scurvy. Give me an orange!

You say, Orange!

The clown lurches away.

You revolve through the front door of the Thing Exchange and into the lobby. Ah, the lobby. How grand, its pillars or frescoes or whatever! How high, its well-crafted ceiling! How long-abandoned, the style in which it was built!

But you have not come here for the architecture. Holding Thing B tight against your side, as though it might leap from your grasp, you hurry across the lobby to the elevator. A sign reads, Things A–Q, Floor 2. You operate the elevator in the usual manner.

When the doors open and you step out onto Floor 2, a flutter somewhere near the center of you reminds you how very badly you want Thing A.

I want it considerably more than I ever wanted Thing B! you think.

Which is true, if memory serves. Although your long-ago acquisition of Thing B brought you mild joy, like the feeling a child might have on one of the lesser holidays, and although Thing B has never until recently seemed unsatisfactory, still this feeling you have about Thing A is brand-new—as a third lung would be.

In front of you is a desk, and behind it a person.

Take a number, says the person.

My neighbor works here, you say. He or she said—

Take a number.

But there's no one else waiting, you say.

There are procedures, says the person. Take a number, and when I call your number, you can tell me what it is you're here for.

You take a number. The person opens the top drawer of the desk, pulls out a hardcover book—*Against Specificity*, by Hannah Foote—opens it to pages 212 and 213, and begins reading, very much as though you were not there.

Time passes.

How's the book? you say.

I really can't describe it, says the person.

Time passes again.

I met a circus clown, you say, who wanted an orange—or was it a magistrate who wanted a job?

Have a seat, why don't you, says the person without looking up from the book.

You take a seat in the empty waiting area, clutching your number.

Your number! cries the person.

You walk back over to the desk and show the person your number.

Very good, says the person. What is it you've come for?

Thing A, you say.

Something retreats in the person's eyes, or else he or she blanches or gives no sign.

Thing A? says the person.

Thing A, you say.

You might consider Thing C, says the person. It's the new sensation.

I don't think—

Or Thing D? True love in a jar, sort of?

No, I—

Well then, says the person. How about—

How about Thing A? you say.

Making a face, the person presses a button on the desk and

says, Got someone here who wants to see Thing A.

Thing A? says a disembodied voice.

Thing A, says the person.

Have you mentioned Thing C—

I know how to do my job, says the person.

The silence is big.

What did he bring? says the disembodied voice.

Could be a he or a she, says the person.

What did he or she—

What's that under your arm? says the person.

Thing B, you say, and you hold it up.

Thing B, the person says, finger on the button.

What else did he or she bring? says the voice.

Nothing, you say.

Nothing, says the person.

Nothing? says the voice.

Nothing? says the person.

Nothing, you say.

Nothing, says the person.

The silence is great with child.

Look, says the person, Thing A is an upgrade. You can't just come two-stepping in here with Thing B and expect to go home with Thing A.

Thunk! That's the sound you'll make when your long slide ends and you hit the box.

What do I need to do? you say.

Leave? says the person.

No, what do I—

Bring us your mother, says the person.

The elevator says, Ding!

Your mother, says the person, plus Thing B. Then we can

talk about Thing A.

The person's face is contorted as though by some internal pressure. Is he or she serious about this mother business? You don't know, but the twisted face reminds you of your childhood—of all the things your mother did to you. She did this, she did that, she did the other thing—what didn't she do? It's a wonder you're still standing.

Do I bring her, you say, to Floor 2?

In your mind's ear your voice echoes: Floor 2? Floor 2? Floor 2?

Whoa, friend, says the person. I'm just messing with you. Desk jobs, you know—got to keep yourself amused. Never mind your mother. You'll find Thing A down the hall in such-and-such a room. Take a left, then maybe a right, then another left or right or what have you. You can't miss it.

Your conscience hounds you down the hallway. Would you really have traded in your own mother? True, your life, thanks to her, has resembled a footrace along an ice-coated sidewalk—a race you, the only runner, are somehow losing. But then your mother's own life has not exactly been an afternoon stroll through a magical forest of European confections. Your mother was born well enough but soon met trouble. She was not a robust child, she could not do sums, and her efforts to please her elders often backfired. She married the wrong man at the wrong time, and, after your father left for Indiana and all that it represented, she had no choice but to work outside the home. She did not, say, swagger from triumph to triumph in, say, the alpha-male world of high finance. Nor would she have wished to, for she would not have found meaning in that world. Nor did she find it elsewhere—certainly not in being your mother.

May I help you? says a helpful-seeming person when you walk through the open door into such-and-such a room.

You want to answer the helpful-seeming person, but you seem to have lost your voice. For there, on an undeserving pedestal at the far end of the room, sits, if you are not mistaken, the very thing you have come for—the thing that is, as your neighbor so accurately asserted, just the thing for you.

Thing A, drums your heart. Thing A, Thing A, Thing A.

To be sure, there are other things in the room. There is, for instance, Thing F, which squats in shame on a pedestal only half as tall as Thing A's but still too tall. Even a child young enough to find the whole world interesting wouldn't look twice at Thing F. Not with Thing A in the room.

To one side or the other sits Thing D, which does indeed resemble true love in a jar. How embarrassing. Your eyes skip to Thing C, which stands on its own ugly legs in the center of the room. Too tall for a pedestal, too angular, and altogether too much like itself: you can see why it is the new sensation. People don't know a bad thing when they see it.

Thing A, Thing A, Thing A.

May I help you?

The helpful-seeming person's words call you back from what was on the verge of becoming a delightful reverie.

Maybe later, you say.

Okay, says the helpful-seeming person, backing away. Let me know if I can help. I do aim to be helpful.

Your mother once said something about the road to hell being paved with the scalded skins of well-meaning people. She said she was going to enjoy walking that road.

Angrily, you thrust aside all thoughts of your mother. Your Type-A blood jumps through your veins, and your spirits rise up, up, up. Thing A! you say to yourself. Shine, O gold tooth! Be zesty, O glorious thing! Make my happy heart leap! Hoo-ha!

And your heart does leap, for Thing A does shine, it is zesty, it practically reeks of glory.

Never in all the years of your life have you seen, or smelled, anything like Thing A. If joy itself were a sugar maple, Thing A would be the syrup joy gave. If contentment were a distant moon, Thing A would be the space pod that took you there. If life were a hundred-mile hike uphill with a sack of bricks strapped to your back, Thing A would be cyanide.

Help! you say.

The helpful-seeming person appears at your elbow.

Thing B for Thing A? you say, rotating Thing B to show off its excellent profile.

The helpful-seeming person looks at Thing B, then at you, then at Thing A, then back at you.

Okay, he or she says.

You experience an internal reaction.

Really? you say.

Quick as a hungry rat, the helpful-seeming person grabs Thing B from your hands, scurries over to Thing A's pedestal, lifts Thing A, puts Thing B on the pedestal, and comes back and deposits Thing A into your amazed palms.

Can it be? you think. Your internal reaction grows stronger and more complex: your lungs are not really trying to dance to a tune hummed by your ribs while your knees cackle, but it is a little bit like that.

The helpful-seeming person guides you to the door. Thanks, he or she says. Come again!

But—

Would you like a receipt?

You don't know why you are hesitating. You know you should take Thing A and get out before the good people at the Thing Exchange realize their mistake. To think of it! Thing B for Thing A, straight up. As though Thing A were not twice the thing Thing B could ever hope to be.

Thanks for your help, you say.

And yet Thing B looks lonely on its pedestal. Different, too—as though the many, many times you've looked at it have not been enough for you to really see it. It has virtues, Thing B does, virtues all its own. It is what it is.

Time to go! says the helpful-seeming person.

Thunk! you think. Will you ever see Thing B again?

But wait—who cares? You have Thing A! You really, really do.

You stare in wonder at the thing in your hands. All at once your inner self starts leaping about like a madman—a happy madman. Thing A, Thing A, Thing A! Your heart jangles against the bones around it.

Goodbye! you say, more to Thing B than to the helpful-seeming person.

No one pays you any mind as you all but sprint out of the Thing Exchange with Thing A under your arm. Out in the street, your great fear is that a bus will hit you, destroying Thing A, or that thieves will wrest Thing A from your insufficiently viselike grip, or that it will rain and Thing A will get wet. None of these disasters occur, nor does any other calamity befall you just now.

Safely home, you carry Thing A from room to room, trying to decide which room is best suited to the enjoyment and display of your new treasure. Thing A does wonders for the bedroom—it brings out these shiny flecks in the wallpaper that you'd never noticed before—but you can't very well say to guests, Come to the bedroom and see my new thing. The kitchen won't do either, for although Thing A makes the spices spicier, the oils oilier, and the boxes of cereal boxier, it does not make the room itself roomier. Thing A deserves to be contemplated at length, by people in chairs, which means that you really have only one choice: the dying room.

You call it the dying room instead of the living room because you have such a good sense of humor. But you are also trying to make a serious point, if only to yourself. What is a room if not a box? And why do we choose to spend in a box the days of our not-really-so-very-long slide into the box? Are we practicing?

Well, it's better than practicing for cremation.

Maybe if you weren't so morbid, you would have at least one friend to invite over to enjoy Thing A. Never mind—you'll invite your neighbor. Oh, and you didn't trade in your mother, which means she can come and see it at some point. But you are not ready to share Thing A with your mother just yet.

You place Thing A on top of the television in the dying room. That way, should you ever feel the need to watch TV again, which seems unlikely, you can do it without letting Thing A out of your sight.

Thing A, Thing A, Thing A.

You sit there in your chair.

Now what? Some food, perhaps.

You start toward the kitchen but wheel around. You're not going anywhere without Thing A. You think: Thing A isn't going anywhere without me, either. You giggle.

It's hard, cooking spaghetti or soup or a pot roast with Thing A under your arm, but you manage. You carry Thing A back out to the dying room, place it on the TV, and sit down to enjoy your meal. It is the best meal you've had in weeks, thanks to the décor.

After dinner, you sit contentedly and watch Thing A.

Look at this thing, you say. Wow!

And so you settle into your new, improved life. When you drink your morning coffee or tea in or out of the sunshine that knifes through your kitchen window, Thing A is by your side. When you delete email urging you to buy or enlarge this or that thing, Thing A looks on serenely. Thing A radiates its figurative warmth into your literal side, against which it is pressed, on the day when, with your free arm, you throw out your computer, your books, and your badminton set—for what need have you now of those? But most of the time—nearly all of the time—you and Thing A sit in the dying room, you watching Thing A, Thing A being watched by you.

You really ought to thank your neighbor for the recommendation. You ought to go next door and say, Thanks, neighbor. Thing A has changed my life! But going next door would mean either leaving Thing A for a few minutes or taking it out into the world, where anything could happen. Another option would be to call and invite your neighbor to drop by—but you've thrown out your telephone, too.

Weeks and weeks go by during which you think more and more strenuously about how happy you are. The ferocity of these thoughts does not indicate that you are in fact unhappy. No: either you are getting happier by the minute or else you just don't have much else to think about anymore. Still, there comes a day when a certain truth starts to tug at your mind, gently but insistently. This truth is a little bit like a child who pulls at the sleeve of someone older and ostensibly wiser. It also resembles a change in tides, which swings all the boats moored in a harbor around to face away from where they've been facing—except that this truth does not turn you around completely. No, the direction in which you are pulled is entirely new to you. You are neither frightened nor excited to be moving this way—you simply move, led by this new truth.

About this truth: It is not that you wish you had held on to Thing B—you don't. Nor do you foresee diminishing returns from your possession and observation of Thing A. You have not suddenly found allegorical meaning in your life, or for that matter in your mother's. Indeed, this truth has nothing to do with your mother. Nor is it connected with your father, or Indiana, or any of the many things that state represents. The truth that roars now in your mind the way a furnace roars in the dead heart of winter has nothing to do with the Thing Exchange or any of its employees, not even your neighbor. It does not in any way involve circus clowns, scurvy, oranges, or out-of-work magistrates. And it certainly doesn't have anything to do with the road to hell, down which you are by no means walking, your hands in your pockets, your feet scuffing the hides of the well-intentioned, your mind turning over and over the question of which you prefer: the little that is or the nothing that will be. There is no one to help you decide.

The Death of John O'Brien

John O'Brien stepped out into a gap in the four-lane High Street traffic. Under his arm was a library book, the novel *Independent People*, by Halldór Laxness. John O'Brien had finished reading the book the night before, and now, under the watchful eye of God, he was taking it back to the library, which was across the street.

John O'Brien's head was full of thoughts. They were his very own thoughts, and he was happy to have them in his head. One of them was that his eleven-year-old daughter, Hannah O'Brien, who could already say "shit" in three languages, might one day appreciate the ironic humor that kept *Independent People* from being too impossibly bleak a novel. She might even appreciate it in the original Icelandic, for all John O'Brien knew.

John O'Brien had never been to Iceland. He hoped—

Just then a terrible noise shattered John O'Brien's thoughts, and in the next instant a dump truck shattered his body.

John O'Brien's broken thoughts tumbled out of his broken head and onto the pavement, where they lay like shards of glass. God, looking down, saw His own face reflected in every shard.

"Thank you for thinking of me," said God.

God didn't really care that John O'Brien had been thinking

of Him. Seeing His own face mirrored in the splintered thoughts of yet another dying man just made God tired. He had never liked His face—and it never changed. Nothing changed. There was nothing new. Everything that happened had already happened a hundred times, a hundred-one times. In the beginning there'd been the Word, yeah, but now it was still there—the same fucking Word. What God would have given for a new Word! But there were no new words. There was nothing new. Every fruit God tasted He'd tasted before. Every song He sang He'd sung before.

Any other god would have hung up his hat a long time ago. But not God. He kept his hat on. He even slept with it on, and then, morning after morning after morning after morning after morning, He got up and faced the day, whether He wanted to or not. Just because the things that needed to be done were the same damn things that had always needed to be done didn't mean that they didn't still need to be done. If God didn't preside, who would? If God didn't look after the John O'Briens of the world, who would? Who, if not God, would set in motion the wheels of justice and light the lamp of human understanding?

While God was thinking these thoughts, eleven-year-old Hannah O'Brien was ignoring the phone, which had been ringing nonstop for twenty minutes. She wasn't allowed to answer it when she was home alone. She wished her dad would hurry up and get home from the library. He always took so long there, which was why she hadn't gone with him in the first place, but now she wished she had. It was springtime, the sun was still up, and Hannah wanted to go outside to play. But that was another thing she wasn't allowed to do when she was home alone—go outside. Her dad said it was too dangerous.

Hannah switched on the TV and turned the volume up high to drown out the phone. She tried all ninety-nine channels. There was nothing on.

"*Merde,*" she said.

She turned the TV off, watching for the final flash of light before the screen went dead. When she was younger, Hannah had sometimes wondered what happened to the people in the TV when it was turned off. Were they okay?

Now, seeing herself reflected in the screen, she pretended she was in a movie. The movie was about a girl marooned on a desert island (the couch). Hannah watched herself scan the horizon for ships. When a dolphin swam by (she squinted her eyes and half-saw a dolphin), she befriended it and sent it to get help. But help was a long way away, and in the meantime Hannah had to find something to eat. She—

But no, that game was boring.

If only something would happen! Hannah thought.

The phone was no longer ringing. Hannah got up and went over to the sliding glass door that opened onto the back patio. The house cast a long shadow across the backyard. The sky's blue was deepening. She knew she wasn't supposed to—her dad would be mad if he caught her—but Hannah slid the door open and walked out across the grass to the maple tree by the back fence. She climbed into the tree and sat on her favorite branch. Next to the maple was a lilac in full bloom. Its perfume was everywhere. Hannah swung her legs and looked up at the sky. It changed so fast at this time of the evening. You couldn't look away for a second or you would miss one of its colors.

Hannah leaned back and breathed in the lilac's impossible scent. Soon, the stars would come out, one by one, and Hannah, if she was lucky—if her dad didn't come home just yet—would be there to see them. What a gift the world was!

The Era of Not Quite

The sun shone, if only to be polite, on a town whose residents were all indoors murdering, by one method or another, the hours of their too-short lives. It was five minutes past noon on a Wednesday during the Era of Not Quite. Soon it would be six minutes past noon.

At nine minutes past noon, Hal Walker emerged from his sagging bungalow on so-called Fourth Street. (It was really the town's fifth street.) In his hand was a single red rose. Hal came down off the bungalow's front porch and stood on the sidewalk, letting the well-mannered sun warm his skin. He slapped a mosquito against his neck and smiled. It was a fine day on which to risk everything.

Everything, in Hal's case, was not much. Although he had a bungalow and a great many books, Hal had no friends, family, lovers, admirers, or even detractors. Also, he no longer had the first half of his life. He did, though, have a job with the local telephone company, deleting from the telephone directory the names and phone numbers of people who had died. It was not a very demanding job. The town had the same eventual per capita death rate as other towns, but it was a small town, so there were relatively few deaths on any given day. Hal spent most of his time at work reading books. He would read almost any book that had a good plot and/or made him laugh and/or conjured up images of the sea. Hal had never glimpsed the sea, but he lived in quiet awe of it. It was vast and moody, according to what he'd read. He liked knowing it was out there.

Lately Hal had been reading novels by Samuel Beckett. Hal was shocked to realize that he, Hal Walker, had been living like a Beckett character—someone waiting around for life to begin or end. Hal didn't want to be a Beckett character. He wanted to be happy.

At ten minutes past noon, Hal set off on foot toward the town library, red rose in hand. He was going to tell the town librarian, Eileen Gallagher, all about the great thing that glowed inside him like a very bright light, i.e., his love for her. And then—who knew?

As he cut across the Unitarian church parking lot, Hal thought about the last time he'd seen Eileen. It had been yesterday. He, Hal, had been about to leave the library when Eileen had said, from behind the circulation desk, "No Beckett today, Mr. Walker?" She was dressed in her usual nearly conservative way, and she smiled a smile that did not, Hal felt, quite exclude him. No one had ever smiled at him that way before—no one except Eileen.

"No," Hal had said in answer to Eileen's question. Then, blushing, he'd hurried home, where he spent the rest of the day rehearsing all the things he should have said—things he would say today.

At the corner of Second (really the third street) and Maple, Hal stopped to admire a bed of daffodils. They looked so nice in the sun, so sharply defined, so much themselves. Each flower was unique, Hal supposed, but to his eye one was the same as another. And of course they would all end up the same: they would become new dirt.

Hal looked at the rose in his hand. What a shame that love required the murder of flowers. Or did it? It seemed to in books, but perhaps in life it didn't. Perhaps love didn't require anything outside itself.

What if love doesn't require me? Hal thought.

As he continued on his way to the library, Hal thought about the Era of Not Quite. According to a book he'd recently read, the Era of Not Quite had been running continuously since the dawn of human history. Human history, the book said, was a little more than halfway over. So was the Era of Not Quite.

Crazy stuff, Hal thought.

At nineteen minutes past noon he stood before the entrance to the library. Only now did it occur to him that he might not be able to speak with Eileen alone. It was a public library, after all.

He needn't have worried. The public was elsewhere, doing the same things it always did on Wednesday afternoons (and with the usual lack of gusto).

Hal went through the door but paused again in the foyer. A vein in his neck was twitching. Would Eileen be able to see it?

A poster tacked to a bulletin board on the wall advised Hal to "READ!"

"I do read," Hal said—and jumped at the sound of his own voice, which he hadn't heard since answering Eileen's question the day before.

Hal considered the rose in his hand: the plush red folds, the desperate thorns. It was not a subtle thing. It was a hell of a thing to give to a woman you barely knew.

Maybe, Hal thought, my plan is not such a good one.

But then an image arose before his mind's eye. It was an image of himself in the future—himself lying alone in bed, unwashed, malnourished, diseased, loveless, known by none, forsaken by all, and, to boot, nearly dead.

Hal shuddered. To pluck up his courage, he pricked his thumb with the rose's nastiest-looking thorn. It hurt, but only a little. A single bead of blood welled up and jiggled there on his trembling thumb like some kind of liquid ruby. Hal brought his thumb to his mouth and sucked the ruby back into himself. Then he put his wounded hand in his pocket and, holding the rose in his other hand, shouldered through the double doors into the main room of the library.

No one was there but Eileen. She sat behind a computer at the circulation desk. When she saw Hal, she smiled.

Hal walked over to her, wondering if his approach made her glad. She was radiant, yes, but she might have been radiant for reasons that had nothing to do with him.

"Hello, Mr. Walker," Eileen said, eyeing the rose. "Who's the lucky lady?"

Her eyes, voice, and face gave nothing away. But it was fate, Hal thought—surely it was—that the two of them had the library to themselves at that moment. Look at us, he thought, together in the house of books.

"You," he said, and he held the rose out to Eileen.

"I wish!" she said, taking the rose and making a show of smelling it. "Mmm... Very nice."

She handed the rose back to Hal, who didn't know what to do but take it.

"Are you taking her out to dinner?" she said, smoothing her checkered skirt over her knees.

It was very warm in the library. A bead of sweat ran down

Hal's spine to the small of his back, where it paused, as though unsure what to do next.

"I cut my thumb," Hal said.

He held his thumb out to her, and together they looked at it. The bleeding had stopped.

"It doesn't look too bad," Eileen said.

This was as close as he would ever get to her, Hal realized.

She turned toward her computer. "Will you be checking anything out today, Mr. Walker?"

"No."

"Returning—"

"No," he said.

"Well," she said, and she smiled at him the same way she always did. "Have fun on your date."

"Yes," he said.

On his way out, Hal hung the rose on the bulletin board in the foyer by jamming one of its thorns into the cork. He stuck it right in the middle of the "READ!" poster.

Outside, the day had turned ugly. The sun was too bright, the flowers were too bright, and the thing that glowed inside Hal glowed too brightly. He felt as if he might catch fire, starting with his eyes. He kept his head down and walked quickly.

In the Unitarian church parking lot, a band of malevolent children ran past Hal, pointing at him and laughing.

Hal flushed. Did they already know what a fool he was? Did everyone know?

As he fumbled with his keys at the front door of his bungalow, Hal started to cry. He lurched inside, closed the door behind him, and sank to the floor, his back against the door and his face in his hands.

"Oh, God," he moaned.

Five hours and eleven minutes later, Hal woke to a sharp pain in his neck. He had fallen asleep slumped against the door, his head at an angle any hangman would have recognized.

Hal got up and, rubbing his neck, walked down the hall to the kitchen. He took a store-bought pizza out of the freezer. Preheat to four hundred. Okay. He took the plastic-wrapped pizza out of its box. He did not immediately remove the clear plastic wrapping. The pizza looked so clean in there. The grated cheese in particular struck Hal as being pristine, as though it were not real cheese but rather the idea of cheese. Hal hated to bring that idea out of its wrapper and into the world, where it would be devoured.

Such was the way of things, however.

Hal ate the pizza at the kitchen table. On the first bite he burned the roof of his mouth, the part right behind the upper front teeth—the part he always burned when he ate pizza.

The next day, as he rode the bus to work, Hal worried the sore spot in his mouth with his tongue. He was so distracted by this new source of pain that he almost forgot about the previous day's trip to the library. As he reached for the yellow cord to signal to the driver that he wanted the next stop, he tried to decide which hurt more, the rejection by Eileen or the pizza's rebuke. Both pained him equally, he concluded. Could it really be said, then, that he loved Eileen? If a pizza-related misfortune could force her from his mind, was she really as important to him as he'd come to think?

"Next stop!" he yelled as the bus roared past his stop.

At work, Hal kept asking himself the same question: Do I really love Eileen? He wasn't sure. Yes, he trembled when he was in her presence, but then he'd always been a shy person.

Maybe the trembling was something he did to himself, not something Eileen did to him. Or maybe it was just human nature to tremble sometimes, out of loneliness or desire or fear. Who could say?

There was, additionally, the Madge question. Madge was a woman who worked in Hal's division of the telephone company. It happened that she looked a little bit like Eileen. Hal did not find her quite as attractive as he did the librarian, and she never talked about books, but she did say hello to him whenever he saw her in the break room. In fact she was the only one of Hal's co-workers who ever greeted him. The others would grunt sometimes when he walked by, but Hal wasn't sure if their grunts were friendly or not.

Today, Hal wondered for the first time: Might he not perhaps learn to love Madge? Mightn't such a thing prove possible, if not now, then at least later?

At half past ten, Hal went to the break room and saw Madge. She reminded him so forcefully of Eileen that he jumped two thirds of the way out of his skin.

"Hello," Madge said as she poured coffee into her *Phantom of the Opera* mug. "Anyone die?"

"Not yet," Hal said.

His hand shook as he held his plain blue mug out so that Madge could pour him some coffee.

"Keep me posted," she said, and she flashed Hal a kind-seeming smile as she breezed out of the room.

Back in his office, Hal sipped his coffee and wondered what thoughts Madge might be having over in her office. Was she thinking about him? Did he want her to be? What did she think about anyway, generally speaking? Did she read at all? If not, what on earth did she do with her free time?

"Walker," said Hal's boss from the doorway. "There's been a death."

He came in and handed Hal a piece of paper on which "Lafleur, John" had been scrawled. Then he left.

Hal switched on his computer and scrolled through the master file of the telephone directory until he found Lafleur's name. He pressed a button and Lafleur was gone. It was too bad. The town had so few French left.

Hal didn't see Madge the rest of the day, and no one but Lafleur died. As he waited for the bus after work, a strong urge came over Hal. The urge said: Now would be a good time to reread *The Death of Ivan Ilych*. Hal had always found the book comforting, especially when he was acutely lonely. When tangled up in small troubles, let Tolstoy lift your sights up toward large troubles. That was the idea, anyway.

Hal did not own a copy of *The Death of Ivan Ilych*. Usually he borrowed it from the library. But he wasn't up to facing Eileen again. So when the out-of-town bus slowed to a halt at the bus stop, Hal climbed aboard and asked the driver whether there were any libraries along the route.

"Dunno," said the driver.

Hal paid his fare and found a seat toward the back of the bus. There had to be a library somewhere along the way—probably in the next town. Anyway, he was excited. He'd never taken the out-of-town bus before.

As the bus rolled along, Hal looked out the window at the desolate out-of-town landscape and thought about how nice Madge had been to him that morning. She'd been so much nicer than Eileen had been the day before. Why, then, did he still feel a sort of ragged elation at the thought of Eileen, whereas the thought of Madge made him feel only slightly more than nothing?

Hal pressed a finger against each temple as the weight of yesterday's humiliation bore down on him. He sighed. Why couldn't Eileen have given him a chance? Was he such a bad fellow? He had a bungalow, after all, and a steady job. He was well read and was not yet old. What more could a woman want?

But no, Hal thought, Eileen was right to hold out for more. She wanted someone who was not a fuckup, and Hal, unfortunately, was a fuckup. For one thing, he was awkward around other people. And he did stupid things like try to give roses to women he barely knew. No wonder people preferred not to talk to him. No wonder children pointed at him and laughed. No wonder he was riding the bus alone to nowhere in particular. No wonder he stood out as a misfit even during the Era of Not Quite.

Hal felt as though he might cry. But there were other people on the bus, people who probably already thought badly of him. That old lady across the aisle, for instance, with her puckered-up face and her handkerchief. Hal didn't want to make a scene. He didn't even want to be in the scene he was in, here in the sad, slow book of his life.

Hal stared out the window at the roadside dirt. He supposed the dirt looked okay to other people. To him it looked like the future.

"Where're you headed, son?"

Hal turned to see the old woman across the aisle leaning toward him. A smile cleaved her deeply lined face. She didn't seem to be making fun of him.

"To the library," Hal said.

"I'm going to see my grandkids," the woman said. "I'd show you a picture, but my purse got stolen yesterday."

Hal straightened up in his seat. "I'm sorry to hear that."

"Worse things happen," the old woman said.

Hal listened to the droning of the tires against the road.

"You have a family?" The woman dabbed at her nose with her handkerchief.

"No," Hal said.

"You should get yourself a family."

"I'll think about it," Hal said.

What he was thinking was that even if he were somehow to acquire a family, he wouldn't have the faintest idea what to do with it.

"Tell you what," said the woman, settling back in her seat. "I never did think I'd end up a wrinkled old lady like this. Not me."

Hal thought he should say something reassuring, but he couldn't think what that would be. He tried to picture the wrinkled old lady as a young woman. Then he tried to imagine Eileen as a wrinkled old lady. Eileen or Madge. But all three women remained fixed in his mind just as they were.

The old woman had fallen asleep. Her head lolled to one side and bounced a bit in time with the movements of the bus.

Hal turned away and looked out the window. The bus was on the outskirts of a town now. The town looked about the same as Hal's—lots of bungalows, some dirt, a Unitarian church. The bus whipped around a corner and then came to a stop at the bus station. There was a library right across the street. It was a cold-looking library with tall windows and marble steps. "READ!" was etched into the cement wall above the front doors.

"I do read," Hal said quietly.

But a strange thing was occurring. Or rather a normal thing was not occurring. Hal was not standing up and walking down the aisle and getting off the bus and crossing the street and going into this library that was new to him to explore the countless worlds stored on its bookshelves. One moment passed, then another, and still Hal sat in his seat. He sat there like a man who wasn't going to move anytime soon, a man who, for all anyone could tell by looking at him, meant to ride that bus to the end of the line, and then to ride another bus, and another, and then to walk if need be, and, when he couldn't walk anymore, to drag himself inch by inch over the indifferent dirt until at last one day he came within view of the greatest thing on earth, the thing from which all others came, the impossibly vast, volatile, gorgeous, and dangerous mother of all creation: the sea herself. And then—who knew?

Hal grinned as the bus pulled away from the station. He couldn't believe it—he was going to see the ocean!

To be sure, it wasn't much of a plan: go to see the ocean and then...? But the idea of the sea's wildness—its relentless attack on the shore—filled Hal with hope, and hope was a thing with which he hadn't been filled since, well, yesterday.

Hal took a deep breath and relaxed into his seat. One could live without love—he knew this as well as anyone—but one must never try to live without hope. Hope was the only necessary thing.

Hal looked over at the old woman. A string of drool hung off her chin and swung in the air. Hal thought about wiping her chin for her, but he didn't want to wake her. He wondered if she'd ever been to the sea. Perhaps she was dreaming of it at that moment.

Hal settled down for a nap as the bus gathered speed. His thoughts drifted to the red rose he'd left in the library. Perhaps by now Eileen had found it and... well...

And so, at eighteen minutes past six o'clock on a Thursday evening during the Era of Not Quite, Hal Walker dropped off to sleep.

Soon it would be nineteen minutes past six.

The sea didn't care that Hal was coming to see it. The sea had its own problems, chief among them the terrific allure of the moon.

Yes, the dry, barren moon exerted a strange pull on the great earthbound soup of life. Such is the way of things. It may even be that the sea originally sent life up onto the land as a way of getting a little bit closer to the moon. Or maybe that is a fool's hypothesis.

What is certain is that the very fabric of the world yearns for what it cannot reach.

Molly Rivers, 85, Held Outlandish Views

Molly Rivers, a woman whose outlandish views were well known to her close friend Sam Bieber, died at 85 yesterday at her home in West Lawn. The cause was chronological, Mr. Bieber said.

"It was time," he said.

Ms. Rivers and Mr. Bieber were next-door neighbors for more than half a century. In 1966 Mr. Bieber asked Ms. Rivers to marry him, he said yesterday, but she replied that she certainly was not going to marry a man with a mustache. Mr. Bieber shaved his mustache, but Ms. Rivers still said no.

"We've been best friends ever since," Mr. Bieber said.

Ms. Rivers' unconventional views were not limited to the subject of her neighbor's facial hair. At a cocktail party in 1977, for instance, she scoffed when an acquaintance spoke of the cassowary, a large, flightless bird that, the acquaintance said, lived in tropical Queensland and could kill a human being with its big toe.

"No such bird exists," Mr. Bieber recalls Ms. Rivers saying on that occasion.

That there is indeed such a bird Ms. Rivers never admitted, unless it were to herself, privately, in one of those moments of self-reckoning that even a woman of outlandish views must, this newspaper supposes, occasionally stumble into.

Molly Eleanor Rivers was born on March 19, 1928, "somewhere out West," Mr. Bieber said. She spoke rarely, at least to Mr. Bieber, about her early life. We do know, because he does, that she dropped out of high school to work in an underwear factory during the war. That American soldiers fought in the comfort of first-rate undergarments was not irrelevant to the war's outcome, Ms. Rivers believed.

"Here indeed is a woman," Mr. Bieber remembers saying to himself on the fine spring morning in 1953 when he first caught sight of his new neighbor.

He was right: Molly Rivers was a woman. She was never to be his woman, though, or anyone else's. She remained her own woman until the day she died. "Not that she didn't have boyfriends," Mr. Bieber said. "None of them worthy of her, of course." Now, according to her own view, she belongs to all of us. "The dead belong to the living," she said one evening in the mid-1980s as she leaned on the chain-link fence that set her world neatly and forever apart from Mr. Bieber's.

"She was wrong about that," Mr. Bieber said yesterday. "The dead belong to themselves. Even more than the living do."

"You can start writing mine now," he added. "I won't last long without her."

Funeral arrangements are being handled privately.

I'm Sorry I Lost the Scrap of Paper on Which You Outlined Your Plans for the Future

Can you really not remember them? You outlined them in such detail. The divorce, the emphasis on whole grains... You were determined to live more alphabetically, as I recall. Or was it more phonetically?

Think: What were you going to allow whom to see you wearing, and when? I know that was on there, and I'm pretty sure it was underlined. If you can get that down again, it may jog your memory. If not, well, lucky you: you get to plan your future all over again. It will be almost like living twice. Have you always wanted to reread "Bartleby the Scrivener"? Or look away, blushing, as the northbound spring caressed the expectant fields of Indiana? Well, now you can, someday.

Look, if you're really so worried about the future—which I doubt, seeing as you left your plans for it on my coffee table—consider that the source of your anxiety is constantly shrinking. You have less and less future to worry about, is what I'm saying.

Maybe it's time to draw up a list of your plans for the past.

My Memoir

I was born in 1971, as though to compensate the world for its loss of the Beatles. In 1975, the year Saigon fell, I fell, too, and cracked my head open on the corner of a brick fireplace. I bled but did not die. There followed a long period of continued non-death. Soon enough, there I was, sprawled (but still not dead) on the lawn in front of the college library, dreaming of mangoes. I wooed my ennui. It didn't notice.

I got a haircut, a B.A. in anthropology, and a job delivering coffee beans.

Time passed, as was its habit back then. In 1999, the year nobody knew what to do, I went to the university whose name is the answer to the question "What color is shit?" and read a lot of books other people had written about what still other people had done to themselves and others.

A woman rescued me and took me to Boston, where love died. Drinking took me up, but its heart wasn't in it. I disassembled my personality, sold the parts on eBay, and used the proceeds to buy a blank slate, which I named after myself.

I wanted to learn how to be written on.

When the World Broke

When the world broke, a certain farsighted county commissioner announced a storytelling contest.

"Whoever can tell the story that fixes the world," she said, "shall be a hero to the people and shall receive a hero's pension for the rest of his or her days."

The county commissioner sighed, for the word *days* belonged to the unbroken past. Since the breaking, there had been only twilight, a perpetual neither-this-nor-that. Schools of thought had arisen to argue whether the world was getting imperceptibly darker or lighter, but the county commissioner had closed the schools down. The world didn't need another argument—it needed a story.

Word of the contest went out across the county. Messengers limped along the banks of rivers that flowed sideways. Town criers whose voices had deserted them held up signboards proclaiming the news. Farmers idled by the lack of sunlight leaned on fences and debated whether the protagonist in the winning story would be man or beast.

"Man," said one.

"Beast," said another.

Finally the news reached the remotest village in the county, a village so small, so poor, so snugly nestled against so forbidding a forest that the very breaking of the world had gone unnoticed by all but one of its residents. The exception was a young boy whose mother had fallen deathly ill. She had not gotten better, even though he loved her very much. That was how he knew the world was broken.

When he heard of the contest, the boy nodded his golden-haired head and said, "I know just the story to tell."

The boy tiptoed into the room where his mother slept. In the half-light of the broken world, she did not look as sick as the boy knew her to be. The gray light softened the jutting bones of her face, and if the boy did not look directly at her hands, he could pretend that they had not begun to resemble claws.

The boy knelt by the bed where his mother lay. "Wake up, Mama."

His mother's eyes fluttered open and she clutched at his arm. "You're leaving me."

"I'll bring help."

"No, you won't."

"I will," said the boy, pulling his arm free and rising.

His mother opened her mouth as if to say something else, but in an instant her heavy lids fell shut and she was again asleep.

"Bye-bye, Mama," the boy whispered, biting his lip.

The boy filled a water bottle, put on his shoes, and took a bag of rolled oats from the cupboard. He stopped next door to ask old Mrs. Luciano to look in on his mother while he was away. And then, on foot, he left what was, to him, the known world.

The unknown world turned out to be wider than the boy had imagined. He walked for what would have been days, walked until his feet cracked and oozed. Everywhere he walked, the boy saw signs of the breaking. Cornstalks slumped in withered fields. Emaciated cows regarded the boy with wild eyes. In every town, the shops were boarded up. Neither the sun nor the moon showed its face, and for the most part the people of the county followed suit.

At the end of a long time, the foot-weary boy crested a rise to find spread before him in the gloom a valley lit by a thousand electric lights, a valley crisscrossed by roads and littered with many hundreds of buildings. The boy had never seen so busy a valley, not even in his mind's eye. It seemed the very center of the world.

The boy sat down atop the rise and tossed a handful of raw oats into his mouth. The city in the valley below was the county seat, he knew. He wondered if his mother had ever been there.

The thought of his mother was like a fist squeezing the boy's heart. He bit his lip but could not keep from crying.

Just then an old man in a long, dark robe shuffled over the rise, leaning on a walking stick.

The old man stopped and said, "For whom are you crying, little boy?"

The boy wiped his nose on his sleeve.

"When I cry," the old man said, "I cry for myself."

The boy offered the old man some oats.

"I only eat meat," said the old man. "It keeps me vital. Are you going to the county seat for the storytelling contest?"

"I'm going to win the storytelling contest," the boy said.

"Oh?" said the old man. He had a face like a gourd. "You might finish second."

The old man had kept his voice even, but the boy knew a boast when he heard one.

"Tell me your story," said the boy, to be polite.

The old man let his walking stick fall to the ground and spread his arms wide.

"Once," he said, "or twice, there was a great fish. This fish swam very fast. If twice, this fish swam very fast twice. All the other fish—fishes?—could not figure out why the one great fish swam so fast. If twice, they could not even figure it out the second—"

"Stop right there," said the boy.

The old man stood as if frozen, his arms outstretched, a mad gleam in his eye.

"That's not a real story," said the boy.

Something was wrong with the old man. His eyes got wider and wider, and then he clutched his chest and fell to the ground and gasped—"Ungh!"—and was no more.

Dead! Just like that.

The boy did not want to cry again. He hugged himself and rocked back and forth on his heels and told himself that his mother was not going to die. But he could almost picture it: her eyes, like the old man's, looking but not seeing him, her son; her hands flung out to her sides in a final gesture that he, the boy, could not decipher.

"Mama," the boy whispered.

Had he killed the old man with his criticism?

After a time, the boy closed the dead man's eyes. He folded the man's arms across his chest and smoothed his robe. He had neither the strength nor the time to bury him, so he pinned a note to the robe: *Bury me, please.* Then he set off down the hill.

Soon the boy found himself on the outskirts of the county seat. People clogged the dusty streets. There were fruit vendors, woodcarvers, paupers, artists, and drunks. There were mothers with children and children without mothers. Dogs snuffled in the dirt while pigeons winged overhead. The boy was almost run over by a fat man pushing a wheelbarrow full of pickles.

"Watch it, kid," said the man.

Everybody was walking in the same direction. The boy trudged along with the rest. His legs ached and his feet did too. As the street narrowed, the crowd thickened. Jammed in there among so many people who were taller than he was, the boy started to wish he had stayed at home. He thought that the old man on the hill should have stayed at home too. One moment, the old man had been telling a story—not a good story, but a story nonetheless. The next moment, he was as dead as a log on the floor of the forest near the boy's home. Like a log, he would rot into the earth.

So that's how it is, the boy thought.

The boy walked among the living under the overhanging eaves of the tall city houses. Soon the street opened out into a square and the procession came to a halt. There was a tremendous buzz of excited voices. The whole world, it seemed, had converged upon this one place.

A trumpet sounded.

"Let the contest begin!" cried a voice.

As a raucous cheer tore through the crowd, the boy scrabbled up a fence at the edge of the square. From his new perch he saw, floating as it were on a sea of heads, a stage, and on it a woman dressed in a navy business suit—the county commissioner, the boy supposed.

The woman stepped up to a microphone.

"Who among you can mend the world?" she said.

Thousands of noses and mouths paused in their breathing.

"I can!" said a man's deep voice.

The crowd parted as a tall, doughy man wearing a suit of leather made his way to the stage. He climbed the stairs at the side of the stage and came forward with the air, the boy thought, of a pompous fool.

"There are four elements," the man said into the microphone. "Earth, wind, water, and tungsten. These elements must at all times be kept in balance, or else the world will break. As it now has broken."

The man paused as though to allow the assembled masses to admire the cut of his jaw.

"From the womb of one yet unborn," he said, "shall be born another who shall beget yet another. This third person shall restore the world's balance. But not in our lifetimes."

There was tepid applause as the leather-clad man left the stage.

The county commissioner said, "Thank you, sir, for going first. But no, your story is not good enough. We need someone who can fix the world here and now. Anyone?"

A diminutive woman came forward. She was oddly pretty, the boy thought, but he could tell from the way she walked that she was a bit cracked. Upon reaching the microphone she said, "There once was a pile of shit."

"More than once," cried a heckler.

"In the shit," the woman said, "was a seed, and one day that seed sprouted and a daisy grew up toward the sun, and it was good. Thank you."

The woman left the stage to a mixture of cheers and jeers.

"Next?" said the county commissioner.

There followed half a dozen technically flawless stories with no heart.

"Are all our storytellers broken too?" said the county commissioner after the sixth of these forgettable fictions. "Let's take a ten-minute break."

During the break, the boy climbed down off the fence and made his way through the crowd and toward the stage. He thought of his mother: how she'd told him once that motherhood had been the happiest accident of her life; how she loved the wild mushrooms he used to gather on Mondays in the forbidding forest; how, during the lean winter months, she would insist that every meal they skipped on earth was a meal they were owed in heaven.

"Kid, are you all right?" said a voice.

The boy wiped his eyes on his sleeve and nodded.

The county commissioner stepped once more to the microphone.

"Who among you," she said, "can mend the world? Be honest, now."

The boy's ears buzzed and he felt a little dizzy as he climbed onto the stage. As the county commissioner adjusted the microphone for him, he gazed out over the sea of upturned faces, each of which now registered its owner's astonishment as a very great thing happened—a thing that had not happened since before the world broke—a thing that was this: A sunbeam slanted out of the shattered sky and onto the boy, illuminating his golden hair.

The boy savored the sun's warmth on his face, neck, and shoulders. Then he leaned toward the microphone and said, "There once was a boy who gave his life so that his mother might live."

The boy stood blinking in the unbroken sunlight. So be it, he thought. Then he began to move.

People later said that it had to be, that fate was fate and destiny was destiny and there was nothing anyone could or should have done. Whether that is true or not, the fact is that the people gathered in the county seat that day made no move to stop the boy from climbing down off the stage, walking out of the square—in fact they followed him—and toward the river that flowed (sideways) through the city, at the bottom of a hundred-foot gorge. They did not stop the boy from walking out to the middle of the Fourth Street Bridge. They did nothing but watch as the boy climbed up on the railing and turned his eyes to the sun, which still had eyes only for him.

No, you won't, the boy thought, remembering his mother's last words to him.

When the boy jumped, the crowd surged forward, half-expecting him to fly away laughing or to land on his feet and give a thumbs-up.

When his body broke upon the rocks and the sun came out everywhere and the river started flowing downstream again, the watchers weren't even surprised—not at first. Then their eyes widened at what they'd witnessed, and many of them fell to their knees while others shouted or wept or berated themselves or congratulated one another or prayed or cursed or called for drinks to be on the house.

"We didn't deserve him," said an old woman. Soon everyone was saying it, and they kept saying it—would say it every year, in fact, as they raised glasses or jugs to their lips on the anniversary of the day the golden-haired boy had mended the world.

The boy's mother was out of bed and eating toast for the first time in weeks when the messengers arrived.

"Your son," they said, their eyes avoiding hers. "He's—"

"You're lying," she said. "Get out. Get out!"

She lunged for her kitchen knife, but the messengers, who'd expected something like this, restrained her. She mustn't dishonor the memory of her son or cast a shadow on his shining deed, they told her. Plus, the county commissioner wanted to know if she would accept a lifetime pension in her son's stead.

It took a few days, but Mrs. Luciano, the neighbor, finally talked the boy's mother into accepting the messengers' message—all of it.

And so the boy's mother was taken to the county seat, where she'd never been before. A fuss was made over her—mother of the world-fixer!—and in time she smiled again. With her new pension, she acquired a three-story house and a taste for the darkest chocolates. But no one knew how to behave around her, no one needed her, and there was no one at whom she could hurl the questions that now formed the hard core of her life: What kind of world required a child's death merely in order to be restored to its usual sorry state? What kind of mother slept while her son went away forever? And what kind of son...?

She refused to finish that last question, even in the privacy of her mind. Nevertheless she answered it, year after heavy year, when, on the appointed day, she raised a glass and led the people in affirming that her son had not been deserved.

Men

A poet was not, to Alice's way of thinking, a serious suitor, especially if his name was Walter Wharton. A serious suitor did real work, made real money, and had a real name—that is, he was a man. And so when her downstairs neighbor, a poet named Walter Wharton, finally got around to asking her out—for a month he'd been tongue-tied when he passed her in the stairwell—Alice, although she had to admit that Walter was more handsome than she'd noticed before, changed the subject.

"Why don't you go by Walt?" she said.

Walter explained that a poet could hardly use the name Walt Wharton. It sounded too much like—

"Think of it as an opportunity," Alice said. "You could grow a long beard, work up a routine. There'd be money in that."

She had meant it as a joke, more or less, but Walter looked hurt, so the next day Alice walked with him up the street to the Last Drop for a cup of coffee. As the espresso machine wheezed in the background, Walter spoke of the heaviness of sunflowers and the importance of line breaks.

"Tell me more," Alice said.

He did, and she pretended to listen. Then she looked at her watch.

"Oh my gosh!" she said.

Days passed before Alice gave Walter another thought, but one evening, on her way up the stairs, it struck her as odd that this man who used to spend so much time in the stairwell was, of late, nowhere to be seen. Had he died? Did he come and go now via the fire escape? Alice wondered if Walter were suffering over her, wondered if poets suffered more deeply than other men. She pictured him bleary-eyed and tousle-haired, three days' blond stubble adorning his strong jaw. Why had he given up so easily? Men who didn't call themselves poets had written her poetry. Why hadn't Walter?

After a dinner of canned tuna on toast, Alice Googled Walter's name and learned that, two years earlier, he'd won a prize from Rutgers University for the best poem about the New Jersey landscape. The poem was called "Pine Barrens, 10 a.m." Alice loved the Pine Barrens, loved the twisted, dwarf-like trees and the coffee-colored rivers. She'd been there only once—in a canoe that almost tipped, and she'd forgotten to put on sunscreen—but still, it was exciting to think that this man had written a poem about a part of her world. And won some money for it.

The next morning, Alice slipped a note under Walter's door: *Coffee again sometime?*

That evening, Alice braided her hair, played an old bossa nova record, and paced around her apartment drinking the wine she had picked up on the way home from work. She asked the hyacinth she had bought herself why Walter, who lived directly below her and could hear her footsteps, had not—by six o'clock, seven o'clock, eight, nine, or ten—appeared at her door. Had he found it so easy to stop wanting her?

Alice frowned at herself in her full-length—and full-width—mirror.

"Men," she said to the hyacinth.

Two humiliating days passed before Walter finally showed up, explaining that he'd been away at a writers' colony in Indiana and had only just gotten Alice's note. By this time, Alice was in no mood for poetry. Walter was not nearly as handsome as her mind's eye had made him out to be—she could not imagine kissing those baby-fat cheeks—and anyway, what kind of man spent time in Indiana?

"I'm sorry, Walter," Alice said, "but I've just started seeing someone."

She watched as the poet retreated down the stairs. For a big man, she had to admit, he moved with surprising grace. Hours later, she could still picture the way his fingers had traced the inside of the banister's curve.

My Foot Is on Fire

Flames curl from the toe of my brown leather shoe as I sit by this café window and think of you.

What are you up to these days, and with whom? Do you sense from afar that my foot is on fire?

People in the café are beginning to stare. They don't like my foot being on fire. They want me to leave.

They want the same thing you wanted.

I'll go in a minute, but first I want to know: Do you care that my foot is on fire? If all of me were on fire, would that do the trick?

Love, if you were on fire, I would bring water.

All right, I'm going now. I just wanted you to know how I was doing.

The Man Who Was Cast into the Void

A man was on his way to the corner store to buy some half-and-half—or "one," as he liked to call it, a joke that pleased neither the man's wife nor their sullen sons—when, just like that, he was cast into the void. He did not fall into the void, he did not fly through it, he did not gasp for air that was not there. No, he was quite simply cast, and then there he was, in the void, without a physical body but with, it seemed, the same slightly dazed consciousness through which his earthly experiences had been filtered.

I wonder, thought the man, if I could just sort of twitch myself back over into the world.

He tried it—twitching—but the more he twitched, the more he realized that there was nothing to twitch. For truly he no longer had a body.

He tried to get his bearings, but there were no bearings to be gotten and nothing to get them with. There was nothing to look at, nothing to smell or hear, no land of which to get the lay. There was nothing to do but think. Fortunately, the man was used to doing nothing but thinking. Life, in his experience, was, or had been, a long string of thoughts, most of which could not be communicated. It was a lonely business. At least in the void there was no pretending otherwise.

But even an intellectual had earthly duties. The one! The wife and children! With horror the man realized that his family might never know that he had not left them on purpose. No note, no phone call, no child support—what would they think of him? What would they say about him to other people?

In fact the man was, or had been, a devoted husband and father. Rare was the day that found the man's wife happy, or even sort of happy, and she never hesitated to tell him that it was his fault she was no longer the cheerful person she'd been as a girl. Still, the man loved her. He would even have said that he loved her sadness. It made him feel needed. He tried everything to cheer his wife up: songs, puns, sex. Nothing worked. He could not reach her across the river of her melancholy. Love was not always a bridge.

Perhaps, thought the man, by getting stuck here in the void I have at last made my wife happy.

This thought did not improve the man's mood. He missed his wife. Also, he missed his body. He missed his balls, as any man would have. And he missed his balls' masterworks, his mutinous sons.

No—he didn't miss his sons. They were even gloomier than their mother, and the man did not have the resources to fight gloom on more than one front. To hell with his sons.

The man was getting sick of doing nothing but thinking. It must not have been true that, on earth, he had done little else, for the monotony he was now beginning to experience was more intense than any he had ever known. He felt in danger of losing his mind—a terrible prospect for one who had already lost everything else. If only there were some scenery to look at, some music to listen to. If only there were anything. The man tried to take a deep breath to steady himself, but there was no air, nor any lack of air, nor any physical man trying to breathe what was not really even missing. Panic rose in the man—but no, it was just the idea of panic.

Am I dead? he thought.

There was no way for him to know if he was dead, or, if he was, whether death would go on forever, or, if it did, whether it would always be like this. The less one knew, the better, the man had always felt, but now he suspected he had been wrong about that, as he had been about a great many other things.

At length the man fell into a kind of sleep.

He awoke, if that is the right word, refreshed, calm, ready to face the day.

But there was no day. Nor was there a night.

And yet there was not nothing. For there was, in the man's mind, a new idea. This idea gleamed like a gold-roofed city bathed in the light of a setting sun. The city had many names. In English it was called Suicide.

Yes, thought the man. It is there that I must go.

But how was a disembodied consciousness to kill itself?

Easy: stop thinking.

The man said goodbye to himself and to his loved ones. Then he threw all his mental weight behind the cart of self-extinguishment. He pictured a void devoid even of him. But no, he mustn't picture it—mustn't think—he must simply will it to be. He must make it so by unmaking himself, but without trying too hard.

It will be a letting go, he thought, not a willed snuffing out. It will be the antithesis of everything I have ever done. Indeed it will negate everything I have ever done. Yet it will also negate all that I never did. How odd. But I must stop thinking!

The man held the notion of his breath. A strange calm stole

over him. He began thinking less. It was good—very good. Soon, perhaps...

But wait, thought the man. Do I really wish no longer to be? Is not a life of mere thoughts—weightless thoughts that can never be shared—still better than no life at all?

The answers to these questions did not matter. What mattered was that the man could not keep himself from asking them. To stop thinking, once and for all, was a feat the man could conceive of but not perform. And so he would go on living, or perhaps not living, in the nowhere he had found. There was no end in sight. He was trapped.

Or was he free?

But that was another question whose answer didn't matter.

In a void, nothing matters.

How terrible it would be to live in a place like that.

What I Did on My Summer Vacation

On the twelfth of July— Johnny! That's enough out of you. You're the one who asked about my summer vacation, and now you can't sit still for five minutes and listen? Remember what I said on the first day: Manners are important to me, and as long as you're in my classroom, they're important to you, too. That goes for all of you. You're in sixth grade now. It's time you learned how to comport yourselves. Got it?

Good. On the twelfth of July I wrote a poem called "Ten Reasons to Hate God." It goes like this:

> Malaria, tyranny, Tupperware parties,
> The self-satisfaction of rich arty-farties,
> Cancer of this and cancer of that,
> AIDS and the fact that I can't find my hat,
> His failure to lessen the pain in my wrist,
> And the obvious fact that He doesn't exist.

Yes, Rachel? You counted only nine reasons? Did you count the two cancers—of this and of that—separately? Well, that explains it.

My daddy's throat cancer got a lot worse this summer, by the way. But I don't want to talk about that.

Raise your hand if you like dreams! I had the craziest dream this summer, right around the time I left my husband.

I dreamed I was a fugitive—do you know what that is? A fugitive? It means I was on the run. I was on the run in a strange country where everyone wanted to kill me. It was nothing personal—no matter who you were, they wanted to kill you. They were weak, though. They had this disease where almost any physical contact was enough to snap their bones. It took a hundred of them to kill you. They would surround you and press in from all sides until they crushed you to death. Thing is, they crushed themselves to death at the same time. Imagine: not only would your death be slow and painful, but the last thing you ever witnessed would be the agonies of these pitiful weaklings. And think of the sound of all those bones cracking!

In the dream, I tried to escape on foot through a dense forest, thinking that the undergrowth would protect me from my fragile enemies. At dusk, a snake bit me on the ankle. "Gotcha!" it hissed as it slithered away. Where it had bitten me I caught fire, and the flames moved slowly up my leg, leaving only ash in their wake, as if my leg were a giant, fleshy cigarette.

I woke up and thought, Where is the joy in my life? Why did you do it, Chip? And Sarah Anderson, where are you when I need you?

But hold on, back up. When I say "Why did you do it, Chip?" what I mean is, why did my husband spend half our vacation money on a saggy-breasted Costa Rican whore when supposedly we'd gone to Costa Rica to fall in love all over again? Can anyone answer that one for me?

Sorry, kids, I shouldn't have said whore. She was a... a sex worker, not a whore. The point is, okay, things weren't great in our marriage—but spending *my* money on a whore? A whore for *him*? Money I'd been saving up for the laser eye surgery I need? Which now I won't be able to afford until next summer?

Yeah, that's the man I married. Look before you leap, girls.

Anyway. Sarah Anderson. My best friend from way back. We used to—never mind what we used to do. We were bad, which was good. When Chip came along, though, Sarah and I grew apart. She and Chip couldn't stand each other. To tell the truth, I could barely stand Sarah myself at that point. She'd gone all New Age and American Zen on us. It was annoying as heck just listening to her talk.

Still, a friend in need is a good friend, as they say. So after Chip moved out I dialed her number.

"Peace," she said. That was how she answered the phone.

"Sarah," I said.

"Jane," she said. "Your voice is all jagged edges and bruised essences."

Normally I would have made fun of her for talking like that, but on this occasion I was too busy blubbering like an idiot. My guard was down, children, and by the time I got off the phone I had agreed to go on a two-week meditation retreat with Sarah at a place called the Center for Turning Inward.

"You are angry," Sarah told me on the way to the Center. "Your husband is a jerk, your father is dying, the globe is bathed in the blood of innocents. You are upset at the way things are going in this ephemeral world of ours. That is normal, that is healthy. Be with your anger, Jane. See it, know it, make it your own. Then let it go."

You mean the way I let my husband go? I thought.

For two weeks we sat all day on straw mats on a cold stone floor. I nearly froze my butt off. Stop giggling, Mason, we all have butts. Sarah had told me to be with my anger, and for ten hours a day, I did just that. I saw it, knew it, and made it my own. Boy, did I make it my own.

Was I wrong, children, to feel that there was something heroic about my anger? In my mind's eye, which did not need laser surgery, I became a shark—a moral shark. I was a vigilante of the sea, attacking only those who deserved it. I prowled the coastlines of the world and ripped bloody chunks of flesh from the thighs and torsos of deadbeat dads, philandering husbands, slumlords, demagogues, and delinquent sixth-graders. The more I meditated, the more I became that shark. My usually cluttered mind cleared itself so I could focus on what had to be done. Sharks never stop swimming, you know. They even swim while they're sleeping. They're all muscle and tooth, and they think a lot about blood, and so do I, kids, so do I.

"Are you feeling better?" Sarah asked as she drove me to the airport.

"Oh, yes," I said.

For years I had donated money to a group called Americans Not Yet Convinced of the Need for Assault Rifles in Daily Life. Luckily, this and all other gun control organizations had failed utterly. When I got home from the Center, I looked in the *Yellow Pages* under "Guns! Guns! Guns!" and wrote down the address of the nearest gun shop.

"What can I help you with?" said the man behind the counter when I walked in the door. He was a big man with big circles under his eyes.

"I need a murder weapon," I said.

"Very funny," he said. "Have you ever held an AK-47 in your hands?"

Of course I hadn't. What did this guy take me for?

"Here," he said, and he handed me the weapon I was going to use to kill my husband.

I had of course heard of the AK-47, but I'd never before seen one, much less held one. It was lighter than I'd expected, and, like my dorsal fin when I meditated, it was sleek.

"Sold," I said.

"Forgive me," the man said. "But I'm required by law to ask you a few questions. Are you a schoolteacher?"

"No."

"Do you have a history of mental illness?"

"Not yet," I said.

"Aren't you the funny one," the man said. "How long do you feel the waiting period for gun purchases should be?"

"Ten seconds."

Together, we watched the second hand on the clock on the wall.

"Done," he said as I handed him my husband's credit card. "Thanks for brightening my day, lady."

Kids, I know what you're thinking: Didn't you buy any bullets, Mrs. Garvey? Of course I bought bullets! What good is a gun without bullets? What good, for that matter, is a marriage without fidelity? Or a father without a future?

After dinner that night I got out the photo album that proved that Chip and I had once been in love. Ireland, nine Aprils ago: our honeymoon. In picture after picture we smiled, arms around each other, like the lovebirds we had in fact been at the time. There we were, on the rain-slick deck of the ferry from Wales to Dublin. There we were, having tea at Bewley's. There we were, perched atop the Cliffs of Moher. But something had happened to Chip's smile since the last time I'd looked at those pictures. As I leafed through the album, all I could think was: At whom is Chip grinning so jauntily in this picture? Had he handed our camera to some bright-eyed Irish rose? And this one—was it snapped by some femme fatale whose lilting accent went straight to men's heads?

I ask you, kids: How much "I don't" was there in my husband's "I do"?

"Ah, Janey," Chip said later that night when he opened the door of his new apartment and saw me and my AK-47. "Has it come to this?"

I wanted to shoot him right then. I wanted to say, "A girl with a gun—pretty hot, huh?" and fill his body with the lead it had earned. But I also wanted some answers. Had the Tica sex worker been the first, or had Chip cheated on me all along? What about Pamela, the co-worker whose silk blouses he'd once commented on? When did he decide that he loathed me—that I was a fungus on his life? Had it happened one morning over coffee, as I read to him from the *Gazette-Register*? Had he had a moment of clarity during sex? If so, sex with whom?

But I didn't ask him any of those questions. Instead, I told him my daddy was dying.

"Oh, babe," Chip said, taking a sip from the glass of bourbon in his hand. "Come in, I'll fix you a drink."

He reached out to stroke my face, but I blocked his hand with the barrel of the gun.

"You're damn right you're going to fix me a drink," I said.

I followed him into the apartment. The walls were bare, and there were newspapers all over the place. I hadn't seen Chip— or heard from him—since he'd moved out a month earlier. It seemed unfair that he hadn't lost all his hair or acquired a limp or anything. At least his home was a mess.

I told him a little newspaper recycling would do wonders for the place.

"You can take care of it after you shoot me," he said.

Right—I was there to shoot my husband. Be the shark, I told myself.

Chip handed me a glass of scotch.

"How much time does he have?" he said.

At first I thought he meant himself—that he'd started referring to himself in the third person, which somehow seemed appropriate. But no, he meant my daddy.

"A month," I said. "Maybe two."

Chip winced as though he genuinely cared about my daddy. Which he did, I knew, but I didn't want to remember that just then.

"Are you seeing anyone?" I said.

"Woman or shrink?" he said.

"Either."

He lifted his glass as if he were proposing a toast. He did that half-smile thing that I used to love, and he said, "We can only be ourselves, Janey."

What the hell was that supposed to mean?

Lucinda? Mason?

Anyone? We can only be ourselves?

Never mind. Raise your hand if you've heard this before: "Guns don't kill people. People kill people." Yes? Most of you? Well, it's true: people do kill people—with guns—often by accident. That's one reason I'd always supported Americans Not Yet Convinced. It seemed like a good idea to erect as many obstacles—Stop laughing, Johnny, "erect" doesn't only mean that. It seemed like a good idea to erect as many obstacles as possible to the accidental shooting of people by other people.

True, when I pointed the gun at Chip's face, it was no accident. I wanted to scare him, yeah. But I never meant to pull the trigger. They should make it harder to do that, don't you think? To pull the trigger? I mean, it's a very big action for a person to take in life—it shouldn't be an accident.

It shouldn't come down to whether or not your hand happens to be shaking.

Thank God I hadn't had that eye surgery. My aim was poor: instead of accidentally blowing Chip's head off, I accidentally blew his left ear off. Blood spattered the wall behind him. There was some cartilage, I think, on the ceiling.

"What the fuck!" Chip yelled. I'm sorry, but that's what he said.

I set the gun down gently.

"Are you fucking crazy?" Chip said.

I picked up some newspaper to stanch the wound, but Chip didn't appreciate the gesture. He lunged for the AK-47 but fell over sideways. One-eared, I guess his balance was off. Still, I got the message: He maybe didn't want me there at that particular moment. Which was fine with me. I'd kicked him out of my home; now he was kicking me out of his. I'd lost a husband and my pride; he'd lost a wife and an ear. We were both lucky, compared with my daddy. I don't know, it all seemed to add up somehow, to make some kind of sense.

"Yes," I said. "I am fucking crazy."

I took the gun and walked out the door and down the hall, down the stairs and out to the street where I'd parked my car. An old woman came shuffling down the sidewalk, leaning on a walker.

"Nice night," she said.

I saluted her with the AK-47 and got into the car.

Home again, I poured myself another scotch and sat down to wait for the cops to arrive. But, kids, they never did show up—not that night, or the next, or the one after that. I guess

Chip decided not to report my little crime. I guess, like me, he figured we were even.

The rest of my summer was uneventful. I sold the gun back to the gun shop. I reread *Lord of the Flies* and grew some tomatoes in the yard. I tried to learn how to make a decent marinara sauce.

Every day I visit my daddy in the hospital. Yesterday I finally read him my poem about God. He disapproved, I think—I think he was trying to frown. The cancer is eating him alive. Think about it. At this exact moment—right now—cancer is gnawing away at my daddy. There is a little bit more cancer and a little bit less of my daddy than there was when I started telling you about my summer vacation.

When I was little, my daddy used to tell me this story about a monkey in a boat. The monkey was lost at sea, but a fish came along, and they became friends, the monkey and the fish. They sang songs together under the starry sky. Then the fish guided the monkey's boat to shore, and they had to say goodbye, because the monkey belonged on land and the fish belonged in the sea. In the end, you're all alone in life. I think that's what my daddy was trying to tell me.

Does anybody have any questions?

Special Advertising Section

Well, here you are, halfway through Douglas Watson's first and last book of stories, *The Era of Not Quite*. What do you think so far? Too many words? Too many deaths? Now might be a good time to take a break, maybe step out for a breath of air or head up to the corner store for a pack of cigarettes. Or perhaps you would prefer to press on, to get the book over with. Either way, before you read any further, know this: the book you hold in your hands offers few of the pleasures of a novel. Were it a novel, instead of being *The Era of Not Quite*, Douglas Watson's first and last book of stories, you would already know most of the characters you could expect to read about in the book's second half. These characters would by now be friends of yours, or enemies. Handing your money across the counter, taking your cigarettes, you would wonder what had possessed the novel's protagonist, in the chapter you'd just finished reading, to send that email she should never even have written. You would be eager to find out, in the book's second half, how the monsignor would react to the protagonist's email and whether the protagonist's brother would discover the rats in the pantry. In short, without even noticing it, you would be savoring the chief pleasure afforded by novels, which is that they help you forget about your own life for a while.

Unfortunately, you are not reading a novel; you are reading a book of stories, *The Era of Not Quite*, by Douglas Watson. The chief joy to be had from this or any other collection of stories is that you get so many endings between the covers of one book. If you are like most readers, you love endings. You love to let a story's final beat echo as you stare for a breathless moment at the white space below the last sentence. This is not bad, as literary pleasures go, but it's thin gruel next to a novel's hearty stew of escape. Worse, watching story after story crash to an early ending reminds you that your story, too, the one you're living, will end, perhaps just a few pages from now. Will anyone bother to listen to the white space at the end of your story? Perhaps, but a moment later he or she will turn the page and start anew, leaving you behind for all eternity.

How depressing it is to read a book of stories.

If only, instead of reading Douglas Watson's first and last book of stories, *The Era of Not Quite*, you were reading his first and last novel, *Hearty Stew of Escape*.

But wait—didn't you read somewhere that Douglas Watson choked last year on a badly formed sentence and died, leaving as his legacy no heirs, a single book of stories, and an unfinished, untitled novel manuscript?

It's all true. But so is this: We, the staff of the marketing division of the Estate of Douglas Watson, are here to tell you that our colleagues in the editorial division have completed what Watson left undone. *Hearty Stew of Escape* is the tale of a man, outwardly normal, who carries inwardly a terrible secret. A secret is a heavy thing to carry, a terrible secret even heavier. The secret on which the plot of *Hearty Stew of Escape* turns is not only terrible but also unusually large and dense, and it is lodged beneath the rib cage of a diminutive, protein-deficient protagonist. Poor protagonist.

Don't care yet? You'll be glad to know that just before he died, Watson lopped off one of the protagonist's legs, rendering him instantly more sympathetic. Watson owed this idea to the writer Paul Griffin, who says he owes it to the writer George Saunders, who has not yet responded to our requests for a marketable few words about the novel but who might well eventually send along something like: "*Hearty Stew of Escape*, the only novel Douglas Watson ever came close to writing, is really quite good. I, George Saunders, think you should read it or at least buy it. Heck, why not buy a dozen copies and distribute them to passersby at the main intersection of your hometown, if, that is, your home, if you have one, is in a town?"

Why not indeed? If George Saunders, whose stories appear regularly in *The New Yorker* and who a few years ago was awarded a half-million-dollar genius grant by the MacArthur Foundation, liked the book, who are you, and who are a dozen of your neighbors, to say he's wrong?

You would be a baker's dozen anti-geniuses, that's who.

On page 72 of *Hearty Stew of Escape*, Douglas Watson's first and last novel, the protagonist falls in love and confesses his terrible secret. It is quite a page, and for the next hundred pages, the protagonist, though still three-limbed and undernourished, feels lighter. Then, on page 172, something genuinely shocking happens.

To find out what, preorder your copy of *Hearty Stew of Escape* today. There's no time to lose. Remember, you could die at any moment. Please make out your check for $22.95 to the Estate of Douglas Watson and mail it to:

The Estate of Douglas Watson
c/o BOA Editions Ltd.
250 N. Goodman St.
Suite 306
Rochester, NY 14607

And then, if you like, light a cigarette, settle into your comfy chair, and read the second half of Douglas Watson's first and last book of stories, *The Era of Not Quite*. Don't do it for our sake: you've already bought the book, and we in marketing don't care whether you read it. Don't do it for yourself, either, especially if you have anything better to do with your time, which, remember, is always running out, even when you're asleep. No, do it for the man who labored—perhaps foolishly, but certainly at great length and to the best of his ability—over the book you hold in your hands. He loved you, you know. He just didn't know how to say it.

Wolves

There once was a boy who loved his mother very much and was loved by her very much. Every night she sang him to sleep in a quavering voice that was, in the boy's opinion, the best voice in the world. There were other things he loved about her, too, but the point is, one day she went out and didn't come home. The boy sat in the cottage he and his mother shared, watching the shadows lengthen across the dirt floor. Finally, at dusk, he went out to look for his mother.

He said to the first person he saw—an old man sitting on a block of wood in front of the tobacconist's and strumming a guitar—"Have you seen my mother?" The old man said the boy should look for his mother behind every door in the world until he found her, for doors were the key to existence. "But what is the key that will open the right door?" said the boy. "Let me sing you a song," said the old man, and he struck up a ponderous rhythm on his guitar and started singing a song about love. The boy had heard the song before; it was a sad song, and he didn't like it, especially the part that went, "To be alone forevermore is a chore." He didn't like the old man's voice, either. It made him think of rotten fruit.

The boy left the old man and went in search of a door to open. He found one at the front of the town's sole church. He had never been inside, and he couldn't get in now, for the door was locked. He pulled and pulled on the cold, iron knob, but all he did was hurt his shoulder. "This probably isn't the right door anyway," he said, though there was no one there to hear him. Off went the boy down the street, rubbing the spot where his shoulder hurt. If his mother had been there, she would have made his shoulder feel better, or made him feel better about having hurt his shoulder.

The boy walked until he found another door, this one the door to the library at the edge of town. It too was locked. But it was nighttime now—what did the boy expect? And what was he doing alone at the edge of town after dark? Okay, he was looking for his mother, but wasn't he also looking for trouble? And didn't trouble find him, in the form of a pack of wolves that appeared suddenly around a bend in the deserted road and moved toward the boy with a swiftness and silence that were terrible and beautiful?

The Purest Note That Had Ever Been Sung

Long ago, when fate governed the lives of mortals, there was a lad whose lot in life was to love a girl whose lot in life was to be abducted by a fearsome dragon. After the abduction, the people of the village shook their heads. The girl should have known better than to walk home from church alone, they said. She had it coming, they said. Maybe she was in love with the dragon, they said, in love with his—you know.

The lad paid no attention to the foolish talk. Yes, the girl he loved was wild and free, but she was no lover of dragons. A lover of all things beautiful and good is what she was. She seldom spoke but often sang, and when she sang, time slowed down and the air grew sweet and songbirds would gather around her and earthworms would dance. The lad was the only one in the village who was not intimidated by the mysterious power of her voice, and she was the only one who would sign his petitions for the establishment of a public library, and someday they would be wed, and he would be allowed to hold her hand.

But now she was gone, and life was not life.

And so the lad gathered the things he would need for his journey—some biscuits, a water jug, his sword, an asbestos tunic—and, bidding farewell to all that he had known, he set off on foot, trusting his heart to guide him.

Day became night, night became day, day became night again. The lad traversed lands gentle and fierce, tiptoed through dark forests, climbed over mountains whose terrible peaks were nearer to the sun than to the valleys below. He dodged highwaymen, outwitted con men, clapped his hands over his ears when he encountered priests. He met the eyes neither of pretty girls nor of soldiers whose hands sat twitchingly on the hilts of their swords. On and on the lad walked, until, at the end of a year, he reached the edge of a great, glittering sea. Borrowing a small wooden boat whose fate it was to be borrowed, the lad set sail for he knew not where. For days, for weeks he bobbed about on the vast ocean, and no wave could overcome his small vessel nor shark devour his ill-fed flesh, for in his heart dwelt love and only love. And because of all that love, and more generally because of the purity of his intentions in life, but most of all because it was his fate, the lad came one day to a jagged rock of an island that jutted up out of the sea like the teeth of some great sunken beast.

The lad piloted his boat around to the lee side of the island and stepped ashore. It did not gladden his heart to see hundreds, nay, thousands of bones strewn about the rocky slope that stretched from the water's edge up to the craggy peak of the island. The bones were beautiful in their own sun-bleached way, but the lad was not one to be taken in by the beauty of bones. It shocked him to think that his own bones would outlast him—that, for bones, the flesh-bearing years were but a stage of life, a sort of childhood, the childhood of bones. Could it be that his bones would outlive even the love that was in his heart?

The lad sensed that the time had come to put on his asbestos tunic. No sooner had he cinched the garment about his waist than there emerged from the mouth of a cave near the island's peak a creature so dragonly in appearance that the lad, though he had never seen a dragon—at the time of the abduction he'd been at home, reading Aristotle—the lad knew right away what it was. It had shimmery, leathery red skin, huge, crinkly wings, an evil-looking snout, legs and a tail more muscular than might have been hoped, and, of course, on each toe, a claw. Its eyes were smoldering coals, and they lit upon the lad, and, loosing a blast of black smoke from its great maw (was that a smile on its lizardly lips?), the dragon spread its calamitous wings and pumped them once, twice, three times, and down, down along the slope it came; soon it would be upon the lad, who, thinking that it would do him no good but that there was an honorable way to die, drew his sword, crouched down, and heard in his heart the otherworldly beauty of the lament his true love might sing over his lifeless body. So this is it, he thought as winged death screamed toward him.

The dragon folded its wings and came to rest some twenty feet from where the lad stood. "There are only two things worth living for," it said. "Do you know what they are?"

The lad had not known that a dragon's voice could be so smooth, so mellow. Did his true love find the dragon's voice smooth and mellow?

"Love," said the lad.

"That's one," said the dragon.

"Truth."

"Um… no."

The lad frowned. "A good book?"

"What kind of lover are you?" said the dragon. "The other thing worth living for is beauty. Love and beauty—all else is secondary."

The word *love* sounded vile in the mouth of this beast.

The lad lifted his sword the way he imagined a warrior might. "Where is she?"

The dragon regarded the lad through narrowed eyes. "They say that no one sings as beautifully as the girl you love."

"Thank you."

"By traveling to this island," the dragon said, "you have proved that your love is true. Now let us find out if the girl loves you as truly. She will not sing for me. Will she sing for you?"

A cocktail of conflicting emotions coursed through the lad's arteries. His true love was alive! But would she sing for him? She sang only when she felt like it.

"She will sing," said the lad. "And when she does?"

"If she sings," said the dragon, "I will let you both go. If not—"

"She will sing." The lad hung his sword once more from the belt of his tunic.

The ghost of a smile haunted a corner of the dragon's mouth. Then the beast's legs were in motion, and before the lad could even think about how he didn't have time to draw his sword again, the mighty creature had caught him in its grip—*oof!*—and borne him up into the air and out over the blue water.

Abject terror and animal joy came to blows at the very center of the lad's being. To be where only birds—and dragons—belonged: 'Twas a miracle! Nay, a disaster! The dragon wheeled around and up and (the lad saw, craning his neck) back toward the island, toward the peak. No living thing, the lad thought, could match the power of the dragon's wings. He thrilled, in a quivering-with-fear sort of way, to the mighty *whoosh!* of their beating of the air, and in every fiber of his third-rate little body he knew that he was utterly at the mercy of this hot-bellied king of the sky, this talking, flying furnace, this two-winged agent of fiery doom.

It felt almost good.

But then the ground rushed up at them and the lad closed his eyes and he was on his feet again and he opened his eyes and it was dark.

"Behold," said the dragon.

There was a burst of flame from the dragon's mouth. The light flickered on jagged stone, on the jumbled floor of a cave, on the form of a maiden—yes, it was she! At the back of the cave, gracefully horizontal on a bed of straw, wrapped in her cloak and in sleep: here was the lad's true love. Thinner of face and less recently washed of hair than when he had seen her last, she was no less beautiful.

If it may be said that the lad was a harp in the hands of fate—a harp each of whose strings was tuned to a different emotional pitch—then it may also be said that the hands of fate now plucked well over half the lad's strings, the notes tumbling over one another in an eerily beautiful broken chord.

Somehow finding his voice amid all the notes, the lad turned toward the dragon, which was still lighting the cave with the fires of its innards. "You have not harmed her?"

The dragon shook its head, causing the flames leaping from its mouth to sweep back and forth across the floor of the cave. This would not have been such a bad thing had it not resulted in the ignition of one end of the straw bed on which the lad's true love slept.

The dragon snapped its jaws shut. The cave was now lit dimly by the burning bed.

"Oh, shit," said the dragon. "I'll get some water."

And the dragon turned and was gone.

So it was that the lad, having passed the tests of time, distance, and, for now, dragon, found himself alone at last with his bride-to-be. He had not come all this way to watch her burn to death. Stooping to avoid the worst of the smoke, he ran to the blazing bed and, protected by his asbestos tunic, ducked through the flames and lifted the girl he loved in his arms and carried her beyond the fire and out of the cave and into the sharp light of day.

He laid her gently on the sun-warmed rock and cradled her head in his hands. Her eyes opened, and the lad fell, as he had so many times before, into the deep, dark wells that they were. Setting morality aside, the lad kissed his true love, even though she was not yet his wife, full on the mouth. So very, very soft were her lips. Who knew?

Indeed: who?

"Can the dragon be trusted?" the lad said.

"Are the seasons of life adequate?" said the girl.

What the hell was that supposed to mean? The lad didn't know. What he did know was that a lad sometimes had to take his fate into his own hands. He helped the girl to her feet, and together they started down the slope toward where he'd left the boat. The sun was hot on the back of the lad's neck as his eyes took in the familiar yet unfamiliar movements of the girl he loved. He found her gait profoundly interesting, he couldn't say exactly why.

The lad and the girl reached the boat without incident. The lad helped the girl into the boat, and then he pushed the boat off from the shore and jumped aboard. It cannot be this easy to get away, he thought.

He was not wrong.

Water streamed and steamed off the livid skin of the dragon

as it reared up out of the sea before the boat. Its wings were spread wide, it gnashed its terrible teeth, flames flashed across its very brow. Its hellish eyes bored into the lad as if in search of his soul. The lad, drawing his sword and standing in the bow of the boat, felt certain that this time the dragon would not waste its fiery breath on mere words.

This is it, thought the lad.

But then the air was filled with a sound so pure—a single musical note—that the lad forgot all about the dragon. His true love was singing, and it seemed to him that the note she sang was the purest note that had ever been sung. The lad followed the note deep within himself to a place where he had never been before, a place as dark and true as the belly of the hungry earth. Hurt is passed through the world from soul to soul, the lad thought.

When the lad returned to the world around him, his true love was no longer singing. The dragon sat still in the water, ashen-faced. It seemed to be profoundly elsewhere. But in another moment it too appeared to return to itself.

"I have wronged beauty," it said, and it opened its great maw and leaned down and bit off its own front right foot. Then, moaning, it spread its wings and flew up to the peak of the island, where it disappeared into the smoking mouth of the cave.

The lad directed the boat around a patch of oily black dragon blood and out to sea. After half an hour during which the lad and his love sailed in silence, the lad said, "You could have prevented your abduction by singing a note like that when the dragon came for you."

The girl kept her eyes fixed on the horizon.

"Why didn't you?" the lad said.

"I had to make sure you really loved me," she said.

And because he really did love her, the lad did not yell at her or throw her overboard or wonder aloud whether she had no moral center. Rather, he held her in his arms, and together they cried softly.

Day became night, and so on.

On the third day of the voyage, the lad and his love had their very first argument. His heart told him that they should steer one course across the wide sea, while her heart suggested another. They exchanged sharp words, but before long he was insisting on her course and she on his. They resolved to steer a middle course, a solution that pleased them both tremendously, or so the lad told himself.

And it may be that the lad and the girl he loved could have sailed on through life more or less in this manner, devising each day new ways of accommodating each other. Or it may be that they could not have done so. But fate, perhaps out of remorse for all it had put them through already, was to spare them this last and greatest test. For on the fifth day of the voyage a chill wind arose and whipped the sea into a frenzy. Storm clouds piled high over the lovers' tiny boat. Then there was a flash, and lightning struck the boat, setting it ablaze. And although the merely natural flames that consumed the boat could not harm two in whom burned the much hotter fires of true love, still it was a very bad day on which to be boatless in the middle of an uncaring sea.

The water was very, very cold. This is it, thought the lad as, holding his true love's hand in his own, he struggled mightily with his three other limbs to keep his head above the cascading water. The cold squeezed him in its fist. This is it, he thought, and as if to confirm the idea, his true love pulled herself right up against him, and they were face to face, their eyes locked, and he held her to him and kicked fiercely at the depths below.

Then the girl began moving her mouth, and although the lad could not hear her voice over the wind, he knew that she was singing, singing just for him, and at last he knew—there in the grip of watery death—that she loved him as truly as he loved her.

And they lived happily for another minute and a half.

Two Country Gentlemen

Two country gentlemen loved the same woman. Neither suc-
ceeded in making her his wife. She married a customs agent and
emigrated with him across the sea to a distant colony, where
she died in childbirth. The child was stillborn. The following
year cholera swept through the colony, killing most of its in-
habitants, including the customs agent.

Because they did not have to work for a living, the two gentlemen had plenty of time to pursue the ghost of their beloved.
Each did this in his own way. The first, an avid gardener, never
married. Year after year he tended his plot of dark, cool earth,
always imagining the eye of the woman he loved upon him.
She admired, he knew, the care he took with his plants, and she
was grateful for the baskets of green peppers and yellow squash
and other gifts he carried from garden to kitchen—a kitchen
that was hers, though she hadn't wanted it. During the winter
the gentleman tended the fire in his fireplace as carefully as he
tended his garden the rest of the year, and with the same audi-
ence in mind. He died at 81, leaving no heirs.

The second gentleman took not only a wife but also the
wives, daughters, sisters, and female servants of a number of his
neighbors. Sex, he hazarded, provided a foretaste of the ecstasy
of dying, and even if he was wrong about that, it was certainly

true that sex was a good way to look for the ghost of love. To know many women was to know all women, including the one he had never known. Had fate somehow granted her a second chance, this gentleman mused, stroking his luxurious mustache, his true love would have rejected the customs agent and chosen him. Meanwhile, his own wife granted herself a number of second chances in the form of affairs. The gentleman could hardly object. In the end, it was his wife who knelt by his bed when he died, at 74, leaving no legitimate heirs.

Speaking, reader, from beyond the grave, the woman the two country gentlemen desired wants you to know two things: one, that no life is sad during which at least one fervent wish is granted (she remembers ascending to the deck of the ship and catching the scent of the lush new country in which she and her husband would make a new beginning); and two, that the soul of her child, who inherited nothing, not even a single breath of air, is as beautiful as porcelain.

The Cave

A boy and a girl decided to run away together, not for love—they were too young for that—but for adventure. They would go out into the world, they said, look danger in the eye, and laugh. Upon their return they would astound the people of their village with tales of their bravery, their cunning, and, if all went as planned, their derring-do.

The village in which the boy and the girl lived sat on the shore of a very large lake. The boy's father was a shoemaker; the girl's mother baked scones and sold them to priests and wayfarers. Neither child found any excitement in the idea of inheriting the family business. Where was the adventure in shoe leather? What was dangerous about a scone?

On the appointed night—the night of the new moon—the boy and the girl climbed out of their respective bedroom windows and met down by the lakeshore. The girl brought half a dozen scones and a jug of apple cider. The boy brought a cigarette lighter that belonged to his father. Wordlessly the two children got into an old fisherman's boat—they told themselves they were borrowing it, not stealing it—and without a backward glance they rowed away into the night.

When the sun came up, the boy and girl were thrilled to discover that they had no idea where they were. The lake was even bigger than they had known, and the shore appeared wild and menacing. It was lined with twisted trees and jagged rocks. The children looked at each other, their eyes bright. They had really done it! They had run away from home and out into the great wide world.

They rowed along the shore, eating scones and drinking cider. After a while, the boy pointed toward the open water and said, "Out to sea!"

"It's a lake," said the girl.

"A big one," said the boy. "Let's go out there and have a look around."

So they went out there and spent the rest of the day looking around.

Dusk found the boat bobbing out of sight of land and the boy and girl tired, hungry, sunburned, and cold. They tried to laugh, but it was all they could do not to cry. They would have been very happy to see the girl's mother rowing toward them with a basket of fresh scones. But no one rowed toward them. They were all alone in the middle of the lake.

As night fell, they huddled together for warmth in the bottom of the boat.

They were huddled there still when daybreak revealed, on the northern horizon—

"Land ho!" cried the girl.

—an island. The boy rowed while the girl sat in the bow of the boat watching the island take shape. It rose up craggy and darkly wooded. Clouds clung to it as though awaiting its instructions. The closer the boat got to it, the more forbidding the island looked. The girl wondered if the sun ever shone there. Certainly it was not shining now.

The children beached their boat and set out in search of

food. It felt good to be on solid ground. They walked through a damp, dark wood, singing in order to keep their courage up.

It began to rain. The boy and girl stopped singing and walked with their heads down. They walked for a long time. The rain was a cold, driving rain. The boy grew irritable, and the girl thought of the dry heat of her mother's kitchen. At length the children came to the base of a steep rock wall. It reared up, glistening, into the low, heavy clouds. The children turned and followed the base of the wall until the gaping black mouth of a cave promised shelter. They ducked inside and wiped the rain from the backs of their necks.

"I am so very hungry," said the boy, looking out at the rain.

"Me too," said the girl.

"This whole trip was your idea," said the boy.

"Was not," said the girl.

In truth, neither child could remember whose idea the trip had been. It didn't matter. What mattered was that they were miles and miles from the small, comfortable world they had run away from—a world that glowed warmly when seen from afar.

"We should get back to the boat," said the girl after a time.

"Let's explore the cave," said the boy.

The girl shook her head vehemently.

"There might be food," said the boy.

"Like what?" said the girl.

The boy shrugged. He took out his father's cigarette lighter. He was glad finally to have an excuse to use it.

Holding hands, the children followed the lighter's small flame into the darkness. The cave's ceiling vaulted up out of sight. A few steps farther in and the ceiling lowered to about the height of an adult's head. The children walked deeper into the cave, which plunged into the earth like a passageway, neither opening out nor closing in on itself. The air grew thick and warm. The boy and the girl rounded a bend and, behind them, the daylight from the cave's mouth was blotted out. The girl saw by the flame of the lighter that the boy was scared, but he squeezed her hand and whispered, "We'll keep going."

As they pushed forward against the stagnant air, the girl's skin prickled with fear. Something would leap out at them at any moment, she felt. Each step, she sensed, took them closer to something best left alone.

A sudden cold wind slapped the children's faces. The cigarette lighter's flame flickered and went out. The darkness came close. It came right up to their eyes and went in. The girl clutched at her breath, at the boy's hand. Not there. Nothing in her hand. She stumbled and croaked the boy's name. Nothing. Where had he—

But the boy was dead, and now so was the girl. For they had wandered willy-nilly into the cave that was death's abode, and death, ever the good host, had welcomed them.

Unlucky children! You should have stayed at home.

And now here is the moral of the story:

Life erupts again and again into the world, chanting, "Yes, yes, yes!" And death, over and over, issues its one-word reply.

Was there ever a more tedious conversation?

Pachyderms

Pachyderms are noble creatures. Their name has Greek roots: *pachys* (thick) and *derma* (skin). A thick skin is a sign of nobility. Whether hooves are another such sign is unknown—but pachyderms have them.

The truest mark of nobility is good judgment. Lemmings, which skydive without parachutes, are not noble creatures. If you want to find a noble animal, seek out an elephant, a rhinoceros, or a pig. Yes, the common pig, humble though it may appear, is, if you think about it, noble. For unlike its barnyard cousin the cow, the pig, being a pachyderm and hence a nonruminant, refuses, presumably on principle, to regurgitate its food in order to chew it again. This to me is a sign of good judgment. True, pigs will eat almost anything—but they won't eat it twice.

Writers are among the lowest creatures and could learn a few things from pachyderms. First off, any writer would do well to develop a thicker skin. Imagine being able to go calmly about your writerly business while the mosquito-critics tried in vain to get to your lifeblood. Second, think of the money saved on shoes not bought, if only you had hooves. But most of all—and I say this as a writer myself—it's obvious that we'd be happier if we could just learn to swallow things and keep them down. Elephants, it is said, never forget; but that doesn't mean they turn everything that has ever happened to them around in their minds, looking at it from every conceivable perspective in order to see it for what it "really" is. They don't chew their food over and over either. For them, and for the other pachyderms, swallowing is an irrevocable deed. If you start mouthing what's already been halfway down the pipeline (I imagine a pachyderm saying to a ruminating writer), someday you'll turn around and find yourself eating your own shit!

Which may be art, but it's no way to live.

Life on the Moon

Well, so there's life on the moon. Little spiderlike things, they say—a marvelous discovery. Nine legs, not eight, but otherwise the classic spider look. Translucent whitish little buggers creeping about on the white-rock face of the moon. Who knew?

Already they have crawled into the vernacular, these "moon spiders." Already, a week after the discovery, it is difficult to remember a time when, for us, there were no spiders—no life at all—on the moon.

I may as well report that I preferred the old, lifeless moon. Life has its corollary, after all. No longer may a troubled earth-bound soul look out at the moon and think: There at least nothing dies.

But I suppose if I were on the moon and didn't know any better, I would look at the earth and say to myself, There I wouldn't be alone.

The Fate of Mothers

The mothers have all been discovered, the dead mothers: our mothers. They are not dead after all. They have carved a city out of ice and are watching us from its ramparts. They do not entirely approve of us. They especially frown upon our desire to go to them, which, in any case, we cannot do.

Krafchak, alone among men, has no need of such a pilgrimage. He knows that his mother approves of all that he does, not because he is her son, but because all that he does is right, and he does it correctly. Each of Krafchak's many ventures, public and private, he carries off with just the sort of aplomb that his mother, though dead, still expects of him. Krafchak therefore has no need of his mother.

We others pity him, just as the other mothers pity his mother.

Narrative of the Life of Jacob Livesey

Jacob Livesey entered the world via his mother during a period of growth in the manufacturing sector and stagnation in the arts. He himself stagnated until a rainy Wednesday afternoon halfway through his thirty-ninth year, when, quite by accident, he discovered that he was a composer of experimental music. It happened in the usual way: the clatter of the fallen spoon, the rain against the pane. In that moment, Jacob heard the world as though for the first time. It was the only time he ever fell in love.

Soon Jacob was the owner of a basement recording studio and a top-floor reputation within the avant-garde composers' community. There were many avant-garde composers (the arts having long ago ceased stagnating), but there was, it was said, only one Jacob Livesey. If you wanted to hear the surprisingly sensual musicality of the everyday sounds of the age, you could either listen for it yourself or you could listen to one of Jacob's recordings. Jacob could put the sighing of a coffeepot on a whole new wavelength. But there was more to his music than that. In his most critically acclaimed compositions, Jacob not only rendered beautiful the quotidian but also evoked the twin longings that tore, although not asunder, the inner lives of many of his contemporaries: the desire for repetition and the hunger for something—anything—new.

Jacob himself was no stranger to these contradictory yearn-ings. He was an artist, after all, and what an artist did was strive, in the most tedious and repetitive way, to break through into new territory. Sometimes the whole project got a little old. Eventually, so did Jacob. Suddenly (as it seemed to him) he had arthritis and emphysema and the feeling, half the time, that he had misspent his life. As a young man he had loved driving; he could have been a delivery-truck driver, making the rounds, bringing, say, the loaves. But no, he'd insisted on becoming a composer—an experimental composer. Of what use were his musical offerings? Were they even all that musical? Did people really like them, or did they just say they did? Had Jacob, in the final analysis (whose hour drew near), contributed anything of value to the human enterprise?

Jacob would sit alone at his kitchen table, puffing on his pipe and thinking these thoughts. But then some sound—a moth thudding against the screen in the window, or a growling match between two lawn mowers—would pull him out of his head and into some better part of himself, and before he knew it he was assembling the pieces of a new composition.

Even in death he pursued his life's work. A few days before embarking on that final journey, Jacob instructed his next-door neighbor to record the shouts and laughter of the guests at his funeral banquet. The resulting work, "Crying on the Inside," won the deceased a permanent place in the strange hearts of the leading new-music critics, who claimed to hear in "Crying" a none-too-subtle rejection of the degraded politics of the age. Talk about missing the point. The point was: Jacob Livesey was no more. He had gone where all others had gone or would go. If the critics had had any sense, they would have said, Go in peace, Jacob, and thanks for opening our ears. What else was there to say?

Author Sentenced for Life

1.

Born on November 14, 1971, Duncan Booth became a writer of modest talent, which he squandered, making his death on November 14, 2071, less sad to others than it might have been, but sadder (this was his last thought) to him.

2.

Duncan Booth was born on November 14, 1971, to parents who, having themselves been born into various degrees of poverty and religion, were determined that their son would be free of both, and so, for them, Duncan's slide into godless poverty—he became a writer—was a sort of half-assed rebellion, one his father correctly predicted would be cut short only by the rebel's death, which claimed its victim on November 14, 2071.

3.

If, in the one hundred years he lived (the first of which came to a close in the darkly comic days following Richard Nixon's reelection), Duncan Booth can be said to have failed at books, he can no less be said to have failed at women, or at least at love, or, if not at love, then at marriage: nearly married four times, Duncan in fact tied the knot only once—and soon afterward tied a noose around his neck, a practical joke (he made sure the noose wouldn't hold) that did not amuse his soon-to-be-ex-wife, whose dissertation, "The Seriousness of Nineteenth-Century Light Verse," shed less light on its subject than on the personality of its author, who did not even find it funny that at the time of her ex-husband's death on November 14, 2071, Nixon, exhumed and rehabilitated, was again running for president.

4.

The high point of Duncan Booth's literary career came with the publication, on his thirty-ninth birthday (November 14, 2010), and at his own expense, of his first book, *The Death of Irony*, a collection of short stories whose seemingly deliberate awkwardness and self-deprecatory autobiographicality tickled the fancy of no fewer than one critic, Yvonne Russian, who advised readers of *The Bottom-List Book Report* to expect "some halfway decent things from the late-blooming Booth," a prediction she retracted by stages in reviews of Duncan's three subsequent books, *The Irony of Death* (2014), *The Death of Death* (2023), and—"Please, no!" Russian came out of retirement to cry—*The Irony of Irony* (2058), the last of which was published by Death-of-the-Author Books, a nonprofit organization dedicated to the indirect euthanizing of aged authors clinging expensively to life in the hope of seeing their words into print, but Duncan survived this act of charity, for in 2058 he was already hard at work on a fifth book, *Birth*, the first sentence of which he finally wrote to his satisfaction on November 12, 2071, the last day on which he could move his arms.

5.

Writing in the December 2071 *Bottom-List Book Report*, Yvonne Russian noted the passing of "the very minor writer Duncan Booth, who obsessively chronicled, in prose that reminded us that long sentences could indeed be written without semicolons, the life of his very minor protagonist, the do-nothing Douglas Watson; Booth hated semicolons."

6.

The sentence whose revision Duncan Booth (b. 11/14/1971, d. 11/14/2071) finally completed on November 12, 2071, a few minutes before he suffered the stroke that left him unable to use his arms or, two days later, his heart, went (and note, again, that this is the first and only sentence of Booth's unborn novel, *Birth*, a book that might well have represented an important departure for the author had his life not been cut tragically short) like this: *"Although I have much to say to myself,* thought Douglas Watson as he fumbled in his jeans pockets for some money to pay the pizza man, *it may be that, like my creator, Duncan Booth, I have nothing of any importance to say to anyone else."*

New Animal

One day in Holland a new animal was invented. It was a miniature racehorse with a jet-black coat and, supposedly, a docile nature—the perfect horse for children to ride. Watching it gambol about the laboratory for the first time, Van Roost, the junior of the two scientists who had produced the creature, felt his face relax into a grin. The horse was his first breakthrough as a professional scientist. Soon the Dutch premier was on the phone, offering congratulations, and in bed that night Van Roost's girlfriend, a public-interest lawyer from Luxembourg, acted five or ten percent fonder of Van Roost than she ever had before. Van Roost hoped that she might now leave her other boyfriend and devote herself exclusively to him.

It was a good time to be alive, Van Roost thought.

Which, if true, did not apply for long to the miniature horse's very first rider, a seven-year-old named Greta who, when the horse threw her, sailed twisting through the air and landed in the worst way and broke her neck.

All of Holland went into an uproar. Protesters encircled the laboratory and demanded that the horse be euthanized. This demand was soon met—by a sobbing Van Roost—but the horse's demise sparked the ire of a different brand of protester. By day three of the turmoil, the premier had tightened child-safety regulations, the Dutch legislature had proclaimed that humans ought not to play god with animals, and the European Parliament had reprimanded Holland, saying its legislature lacked the authority to weigh in on so lofty a matter. Then came the girl's memorial service, attended by neither Van Roost nor the senior scientist. Both men ought to have been there—public-opinion polls were clear on that point—but the opinion of the police had been that their safety could not be guaranteed. Van Roost stayed at home the day of the service with the blinds drawn and a recording of tropical surf playing on an endless loop.

Just when it seemed as though the furor over the girl's death would never die down, it did. A few days after the memorial service, some new scandal, something to do with finance or a crashed plane, diverted the public, leaving Van Roost to confront, for starters, the unprecedented difficulty he was having making love to his girlfriend. They tried all kinds of positions, some from Luxembourg, some from Holland, some from other E.U. countries. Nothing worked, not even the position his girlfriend called the raptor. Finally one day she told him that she had decided to devote herself completely to her other boyfriend.

"What about me?" Van Roost said, and then he thought how pretty she was when she smiled sadly and apologetically and a little bit impatiently.

The next day, an E.U. regulatory commission scolded Van Roost and the senior scientist for their "negligence if not outright recklessness" and suspended for one year their scientific licenses. Muttering that the girl's death hadn't been their fault, the senior scientist packed his bags and emigrated to America to work for a pharmaceutical company. But it *was* our fault, Van Roost said to himself. The bureaucrats indicated that he could spend his year away from science either doing community service or studying philosophy at the university in the town where he lived. Van Roost, who didn't know any better, chose the latter course.

The first philosopher he was asked to read was a Scot named David Hume. Hume was, or had been, at pains to prove that it couldn't be proved that the sun, on any given day, was a whit more likely to rise than not to rise. What nonsense! Van Roost thought as he slammed the book closed.

Many nights, instead of doing the required reading, Van Roost would open a bottle of red wine and sit in his kitchen rereading the newspaper stories he'd clipped about the girl who'd died. Greta. Though just seven, she had already begun a serious study of the flute, the papers said. They had all put the same photo on the front page, a photo of this grim-faced child holding a flute to her mouth, her wispy blond hair sticking out in all directions as though it were trying to get away from her. She was playing, according to the papers, one of Mozart's melodies for young people. Van Roost went out and bought a CD of these melodies. He listened to it only once, and that just halfway through. He had never liked classical music, and even these simple melodies struck him as still being classical music. It actually helped him, for a brief moment, feel a little less bad about what had happened, thinking that however many times these melodies had been played in the world and would be played until the end of time, that number would be the tiniest bit lower now, thanks to the miniature horse he had helped invent. Of course, this thought was insane, and Van Roost felt bad about having come up with it.

Another thing he felt bad about was that he couldn't help noticing, from the newspaper photos, that Greta's mother was very attractive. Her thin, pretty, intelligent face was beset by a tangle of blond hair. In the photo Van Roost liked best, she clung to her broad-shouldered husband, whose face was cut in half by the edge of the photo, and looked directly at the camera. Van Roost felt that she was not looking at just anyone: she was looking at him. Had it really been necessary, her eyes were saying, to invent a miniature racehorse? Yet there was also a trace of humor in her face, he thought, humor or resignation—perhaps around the mouth, Van Roost wasn't sure. Maybe he was reading too much into the photo. At any rate, she was pretty.

He wanted to tell her how sorry he was about what had happened. He even pictured himself knocking on her door, telling her in person. But it wasn't *her* door, it was *their* door, and anyway, he thought as he looked up the address in the phone book and scribbled it on a scrap of paper that he tucked into his jacket pocket, it was unlikely that these people had any desire to hear from him. Surely they just wanted to move on.

Van Roost tried to move on too. He'd been a philosopher-in-training for a month now, and his first examination was nearly upon him. Did death, his professors wanted to know, give meaning to life, or did it strip life of meaning, or did it have some other, totally surprising effect, something no one but Kierkegaard could have anticipated? Van Roost had no idea. He hadn't even realized the class had moved on to Kierkegaard. He went in search of the work in question, a collection of the Dane's essays the editors had titled *Kierkegaard: Necessary*, but the library's copies were all checked out, and the three bookstores in town were also out of stock.

With the illicit glee of a sentry abandoning his post, Van Roost absconded from university life and tried, for a week, to become a drunk and an idler. For seven days and nights, he idled along the edge of a dock by the canal that cleaved the town's heart in two. He drank gin, because why not? When he finished a bottle, he tossed it in the canal, an extremely un-Dutch thing to do. No one seemed to care. Hour after hour Van Roost lay curled upon the dock next to the languid waters of the canal, in whose surface the unthreatening clouds overhead were reflected. It was crushingly boring, he decided, being a drunk and an idler. Still, he finished out his seven days in good faith.

When the week was over, he went home, washed himself, ate a tremendous breakfast of eggs with chives and thick white toast, drank three mugs of strong, black coffee, and then set out on foot to see if he could reacquaint himself with the world outside his skull. This would take a bit of time, he soon realized. Day after day he walked through town, never toward the university, never toward his old laboratory, never, indeed, anywhere in particular, or so he thought. It was spring. Everywhere he walked, Van Roost saw children running, biking, shouting, crying, throwing dirt at one another—all the things children did in the spring. This was on nice days. On rainy days, he was one of a legion of adults walking through the town under umbrellas of various hues. His was black. Greta, the girl Van Roost's horse had killed, would never join this adult legion. She would never get to choose an umbrella color. Not that being an adult was so great, Van Roost thought, but at least he, and these other adults walking around with their umbrellas, had had a chance to discover that. Greta was not even able to discover what her fellow children were talking about this spring. Walking past the playground in her neighborhood—for his steps took him more and more often down streets near the one on which her parents presumably still lived—Van Roost would wonder whether any of the children he saw had known Greta.

Did they see guilt written in his gait as he walked by? Did they, or might their parents, recognize him from the newspaper stories at the time of the accident?

It made Van Roost sad to watch the children playing. He had once been as happy and carefree as they seemed to be, or at least that was how he remembered his childhood. Don't grow up, he wanted to say to them—then flinched, thinking just how tainted a piece of advice that would have been, coming from the inventor of a child-killing horse.

So. One Thursday, after a lunch of cream cheese and cucumbers on pumpernickel, Van Roost set out on not just any walk but, he knew, the walk that would lead him to the front door of Greta's parents' house. It was a brilliant day, one of those blue-sky wonders when, after a night of rain, the world seemed freshly scrubbed and brighter and lovelier than one remembered was possible. But so many things were possible, Van Roost said to himself as he walked along a sidewalk strewn with damp cherry blossoms knocked down overnight by the rain. Looking at the cherry petals, he recalled a scene from an art film a young woman whose attentions he had once craved had made. In the scene, a man gets on a subway car, the floor of which is strewn with flower petals. Someone has dropped a bouquet of flowers and simply left it there. The man takes a seat, and as he rides, listening to the clatter of the train wheels along the tracks, he thinks, in voice-over and without knowing why, that the flower petals are a sign that someone somewhere has died.

Van Roost couldn't remember how the film had ended or even whether the young woman had finished the project. It didn't matter now, he thought as he turned into the narrow side street on which he hoped, or feared, Greta's parents still lived.

It hadn't really ever mattered, he thought. The street was lined with two-story brick row homes with tile roofs. Van Roost's steps slowed as he neared number 64, Greta's parents' house. It was a house just like the others. Pansies—not Van Roost's favorite flower—grew in wooden boxes below the windows to either side of the black front door. Didn't pansies have something to do with death in some cultures? Hadn't he read that somewhere? Or was it love they symbolized?

Van Roost stood on the sidewalk, thinking he should really be somewhere else—at home, for instance, getting his life up and running again.

But, no, this was his life. He had come here to apologize, and he was going to go through with it.

He took a deep breath and went up to the black door and knocked.

After a moment the door swung inward, and there she was, Greta's mother. She was shorter than Van Roost had imagined her, which meant that her husband, who'd stood beside her in that newspaper photo, was also shorter than he'd supposed. She wore a red cardigan over a flower-print blouse over smallish breasts, and her jeans revealed a trim figure. Her thick blond hair was perhaps a half-measure beyond stylish disarray. The shadows under her eyes must have been attributable, Van Roost thought, to the grief he'd caused her.

"Yes?" she said, looking at him far more guardedly than she had in the newspaper photo.

"Mrs.—" Van Roost said, and with a kind of horror he discovered that he'd forgotten the family's name. So he said, "You're Greta's mother."

The woman recoiled, raised a hand along the door's edge. But she didn't close the door. Her eyes (gray-green, as Van Roost had been unable to tell from the newspaper) held his, and her mouth curled slightly, though she was not smiling.

"You're one of those scientists," she said.

Not this year, I'm not, Van Roost wanted to say. He wanted to say, I'm sorry, I'm sorry. He glanced away up the street and thought, My god, this is real, isn't it? A breeze moved through the cherry trees, and the dappled light danced on the sidewalk.

Greta's mother's hand brushed his forearm. He turned toward her, and she smiled politely and said, "Come in."

"I hope it's no trouble," he managed to say.

She held the door for him, and he followed her into a small sitting room whose walls were lined with books. He accepted an offer of coffee, and she disappeared through a doorway to the kitchen. There was no sign of the husband. Van Roost sat down in a leather-upholstered chair in the corner of the room. He could still feel where she'd touched his arm. He scanned the room for photographs of the dead child but didn't see any. There was nothing on the walls but bookshelves and nothing on the shelves but books—serious books. Plato, Heidegger, Proust. A whole shelf of Sontag. Oh, and there it was, *Kierkegaard: Necessary*, the book Van Roost had needed for his philosophy exam.

Greta's mother came into the room holding two mugs. She asked him how he took his coffee. Black, he said. She handed him one of the mugs and then sat down in a chair opposite his, on the other side of a coffee table cluttered with books and papers. A slender volume called *Grief, Sex, and You* caught Van Roost's eye. Greta crossed her legs, sipped her coffee, and looked at Van Roost—again, guardedly, he thought—then looked away, possibly at a clock he couldn't see in the next room.

He blew on his coffee. Surely there was a right way to begin this conversation. He took a sip of the coffee. It was a dark roast, bitter and strongly brewed, just the way he liked it.

"Good coffee," he said, raising the mug as though he'd said, To your health.

Greta's mother nodded, frowning slightly, or perhaps Van Roost imagined the frown because of his anxiety. He crossed one leg over the other, then noticed that his foot was jiggling. He uncrossed his legs and was on the point of telling Greta's mother that he'd been looking for the very Kierkegaard volume she had on her shelf when he heard himself say, instead, "Your husband is not in?"

"No."

Will he be away long? Van Roost wanted to say, and: Is he gone for good? Heat washed over him; he was blushing. He thought about telling Greta's mother that his girlfriend, a public-interest lawyer from Luxembourg, had left him for another man and that he imagined she regretted it. He didn't really imagine any such thing, but he thought it would sound good.

Greta's mother began smoothing her right hand along the top of her right thigh, down toward the knee and then back up again, down, then up.

Van Roost sat up straighter and said, "I came to say how sorry I am for what happened."

Her eyes met his. Her mouth, when it smiled, surprised Van Roost. If I were in her shoes, he thought, I certainly wouldn't be smiling. A little pocket of gladness opened up in his chest, a little bubble of expectation.

"I'm Emma," she said, extending a hand.

That was all. Not thank you, not it wasn't your fault, not get out of here this instant.

"Van Roost," Van Roost said.

Her grip was firm and her hand warm.

Van Roost sipped his coffee, which was cooling. Emma. What a pretty name.

"I want you to know," he said, leaning forward a little, "that it was considered highly unlikely that the horse would exhibit such severe skittishness."

Greta's mother—Emma—looked darkly away and ran a hand through her hair, which really was quite a tangle. "Please," she said in a thick voice. "Talk about something else."

Shame lanced through Van Roost. He blew on his coffee forcefully enough that a drop splashed over the rim and onto his hand. It wasn't hot enough to burn. The husband could come through the front door at any moment, Van Roost thought. What would he think to find the two of them sitting together in awkward silence? Once more Van Roost's eyes settled on *Kierkegaard: Necessary.* He wondered if Emma were familiar with Kierkegaard's position on death. He wasn't about to ask, though, and anyway she had drained the last of her coffee and now leaned forward to place the empty mug on the coffee table between them. Her bra was turquoise, Van Roost saw as she bent toward him, or at least the edge of it was.

"May I show you Greta's room?" Emma said, rising.

Okay, but—why? Van Roost thought as he followed her down a carpeted hallway. He liked the way she held her shoulders when she walked: she thrust them back in a way that seemed to him very proper.

She stopped in the doorway to a small bedroom. Van Roost came up beside her. Sunlight slanted through a window at the far end of the room and glinted off—Christ, Van Roost thought, it's the girl's flute. It lay across a desk in the farthest corner of the room, the sun upon it like a spotlight, but of course one didn't want to think of a spotlight, there being no Greta to pick up the flute and perform. Nearer at hand was a twin bed, and Van Roost registered a second shock when his eyes took in the collection of stuffed horses arrayed on the white bedspread. Beside the bed stood an antique dresser, on top of which sat, there was no way not to notice, an urn—presumably (Van Roost couldn't block the thought) no more than half full.

"She loved horses," Emma said, and then, smiling sadly up at Van Roost, she took his right hand and placed it squarely upon her left breast.

The air caught in Van Roost's throat. Emma's eyes shone darkly, and she leaned into his body, which offered its own response even as his mind jumped away. Look at her eyes, he thought. And he had a point, they were quite extraordinary, they were eyes you could study for a long time without understanding what was going on behind them. The eyes were what Van Roost would remember later, their luminous opacity, and not, say, the breast in his hand, whose feel he was, in any case, too agitated to pay much attention to.

What did command his attention was his rising panic as this woman with married hand began fumbling with his belt buckle. She's crazy, he told himself as she undid the buckle and the top button of his jeans and tugged at the zipper—which caught—and in the next moment he fled down the hallway, zipping and buckling as he went, and out into the sitting room, where, scarcely slowing his stride, he grabbed, for reasons that were unknown to him, the Kierkegaard volume, and then he clambered out the door and, running, looked back at the pansies under the windows (danger was what they symbolized, he decided) and then ran up the street to the end of the block and rounded the corner and slowed to a walk, his ragged breathing splitting the tranquil air of the quiet street, the sort of street on which nothing was supposed to happen.

Walking home, he crushed underfoot the cherry petals strewn wantonly everywhere.

That night, safely housed behind double-locked door and with a bottle of red wine open on the table before him, Van Roost considered what he had to fear from Emma or her husband. It seemed to him there were three possibilities. One of them was that he had nothing to fear. The second was that the husband might try to hurt him, and the third was that Greta's mother might tell the newspapers that one of the scientists who'd killed her daughter had showed up unannounced at her home and made a pass at her.

All of Holland will believe her, he thought.

He got up from the table and crossed the room to the stereo. He put on his tropical-surf recording, and then he sat down and refilled his wine glass. *Kierkegaard: Necessary* glared up at him from the table where he'd laid it. He'd stolen it, he realized with a start. Why had he done a thing like that? He had never stolen anything before. Was he really that curious to know what Kierkegaard thought about death?

Van Roost opened the book at random and read: "Is despair an excellence or a defect?"

Strange question. Van Roost listened some more to the ocean waves breaking. It occurred to him that the sound had no meaning—it was just the sound energy made when, having moved through water, it continued moving through earth and air. Despair was a kind of energy, Van Roost decided. It spread outward from its source in waves. It was probably a defect, but it was hard to avoid. He read on:

Purely dialectically, it is both. If only the abstract idea of despair is considered, without any thought of someone in despair, it must be regarded as a surpassing excellence. The possibility of this sickness is man's superiority over the animal, and this superiority distinguishes him in quite another way than does his erect walk, for it indicates infinite erectness or sublimity, that he is spirit. The possibility of this sickness is man's superiority over the animal; to be aware of this sickness is the Christian's superiority over the natural man; to be cured of this sickness is the Christian's blessedness.

Van Roost closed the book. He got up and went out into the living room and over to the window. Outside, the evening light—energy filtered through dust and water vapor—slanted across the neatly swept sidewalks and against the modest brick homes of the street. Van Roost hadn't known that Kierkegaard was so determined a Christian. He hadn't known anything else about the man either, except that he was Danish and dead, but this new knowledge filled Van Roost with despair. No doubt he was being unfair to Kierkegaard (just as, he'd read somewhere, Kierkegaard had been unfair to Schlegel)—after all, you couldn't judge a writer by a single paragraph—but to watch a great thinker retreat into the waiting arms of dogma was depressing.

Emma's pass at him that afternoon was depressing too, Van Roost thought as he turned away from the window. He thought: No one knows what to do about death. Emma lost her daughter and doesn't know what to do; Kierkegaard peered into the void and didn't know what to say; and I?

I don't know what to do about life, he thought.

He went over to the table and corked the wine. He felt he'd been right to flee Emma's touch and her house, but he wondered, a bit, whether he mightn't have run away at least in part because his most recent attempts at lovemaking, with the public-interest lawyer from Luxembourg, had gone so poorly.

"Fuck it," he said out loud for some reason. He walked over to the stereo and replaced the tropical-surf recording with an album by a Belgian rock band he liked. Guitar chords jolted into the room, and Van Roost began jumping around like a teenager. "Give me some money or I'll give you my soul!" the band members shouted in unison. Van Roost shouted along with them. For the first three songs he was a madman, grinning, shouting, jumping around. Then he got tired and, no longer smiling, sat on the couch as the drums and guitars punched and stabbed the air.

When the album ended, Van Roost didn't get up to put another one on. He didn't get up for hours. Deep into the night he sat listening to the faint buzzing in his ears. He felt he was waiting for something.

The Messenger Who Did Not Become a Hero

There was a messenger who was stuck working for a no-good king. That the king was no good had been proved by numerous studies. His intentions may have been good, but results-wise, he was not good. The delivery of kingly services to subject/consumers had grown markedly less efficient since the death of the old king. Also, the new king was not really handsome enough to be a king. He was duke material at best, according to the studies.

For a distinguished messenger nearing the end of his career, it was embarrassing to be working for so mediocre a king. Whenever the messenger told people about the dozens of professional awards he had won over the years, he made sure to emphasize that he had won them in the service of the old king. Sometimes he grew misty-eyed at the thought of the good old days. How proud he had been, once upon a time, to rap upon doors across the land and say, "Message from the king!" How handsome he had felt, and how efficient, working for so handsome and efficient a king. How certain he had been that his work mattered, that he was helping nudge society ever so slightly forward.

Now, when the messenger rapped upon doors, he was greeted with indifference or outright hostility. Nobody wanted to hear from the new king, it seemed. That, or people were annoyed not to have heard from him sooner. On one occasion, the messenger was even made to wait while the recipient of a message scrawled an angry reply, saying, "Take this to the king!" King's messenger had never been a two-way job before. The messenger would have quit if he hadn't been so close to his life-goal, which was to own the brick walls and tile roof that kept the weather out of his living room, which he also wanted to own. It was a better life-goal than some, the messenger felt, and—in part because he had never had a wife or, even more expensive, children—he needed only another three years' savings to attain it.

It was not to be, however.

Within a year of the old king's death, the people of the capital took to the streets to demand a change. Nothing would satisfy them, they said, but that the new king step down, or else that he get better at his job. The messenger agreed heartily with the second demand, but the first offended his sense of order. Even a lousy king was still a king, he reasoned, and the one thing a king must never do was step down, unless he wanted to.

It didn't matter what the messenger thought. Barricades went up, feelings ran high, and the job of king's messenger became, if not dangerous, then not easy either. The messenger had to take absurdly roundabout detours through the city to get past the barricades; and anyway, very few people at this point were accepting messages from the king. Soon the king stopped communicating with his subjects altogether.

To stave off ennui, the idled messenger drank twice as much coffee as usual.

Coffee was the messenger's one true joy in life. No one in the kingdom knew more about coffee than he did—which was saying something, because this particular kingdom was a kingdom of coffee aficionados. The messenger had yellow teeth. He had drunk tens of thousands of cups of coffee over the course of his life, which was almost over, plus quite a bit of espresso. The yellow teeth were unsightly, but they were not the reason the messenger had never taken a wife. He had never taken a wife because he had never fallen in love.

On the thirteenth day of the protests, the king burst into the messenger's living room with a message in his hand and said, "Take this to the captain."

The messenger bowed, put the message in his pocket, and went out into the chaotic streets. The king's subjects were everywhere, acting like citizens. The messenger walked with his head down and did not make eye contact with anyone. He tried to take the back way to the barracks where the captain was stationed, but the back way was barricaded. So was the front way. The messenger wasn't sure what to do. He kept walking. Then he rounded a corner and fell in love.

A woman stood atop the barricade that blocked the street into which the messenger had just turned. She was not conventionally beautiful, this woman, but then neither was life. The woman had wispy brown hair and so on. A rabble had gathered at the foot of the barricade to hear speeches by the protesters. The messenger now joined this rabble.

The wispy-haired woman stood next to the speechmaker of the moment, a thin, humorless man whose face twitched whenever the word *king* came out of it. The woman seemed bored, and the messenger loved her for this. She had a look on her face that said: Sure, the protests are worthwhile, but the future isn't going to be all that different from the present, and the sooner it gets here, the sooner I can get back to what really matters. (Which would be her work, the messenger supposed, or her private pleasures, all of them simple: coffee, books, modern architecture. She would be a voracious lover, of course.)

All this the messenger divined at a glance.

When the day's orations had subsided, the messenger was able to get close enough to the barricade to speak to his lover-to-be.

"Join me for dinner?" he said.

The woman peered down at him. "Aren't you the king's messenger?"

He had been the king's messenger all his adult life. It was how he defined himself, how he distinguished himself from other human beings. They did other things; he delivered messages for the king. But now he was in love and didn't give a damn about anything else.

"Not anymore," he said.

To prove that he meant it, the messenger took from his pocket the message the king had given him and tore it into very small pieces, which he let fall to the ground like so much confetti. It was the first brave act of his life.

"Who was that message for?" said the woman.

"It was nothing important," said the messenger, although he knew as well as anyone that a message from the king to the captain of his army was by definition important, especially at a time of political unrest.

"You could have spied for us," said the woman. "Now you're just going to get into trouble."

The messenger didn't care whether he got into trouble or not. Nothing mattered except keeping this woman's attention.

"I'm not cut out for spying," he said.

"What are you cut out for?" said the woman, and by her smile, which was a little bit lopsided, although not in a bad way, the messenger knew she was flirting with him.

"Dinner," he said.

They went to Betty's Noodle Shop on Fourth Street. The noodles were very good. Later they made love—the messenger and the woman—with an intensity that surprised them both.

And how did the messenger feel, falling in love for the first time at the advanced age that was his? He felt more or less the way anyone feels who falls in love at any age. Life, until now, had been a mere prelude to itself, he felt. Life would henceforth be a lot of things it had not hitherto been.

But this is not a love story.

It is a philosophical story with a surprise ending.

The messenger joined the resistance. He stood now atop the very barricade on which he had first glimpsed the woman who, by crying naked in his arms night after night, was teaching him what it was to live. He stood as close to her as he could without seeming to want to subordinate the political to the personal. He stood from dawn to dusk, and then, if the woman kept standing, he stood there with her until midnight, even though he sometimes got a pain in his lower back.

More and more people gathered at the barricades each night. The leaders of the movement began to glow with confidence. Surely the king would accede to their demands, they thought, glowing, now that these demands issued in unison from so many mouths. The leaders even offered to put the king through a ten-week job-training course at the people's expense, if only the king would agree to it. There was a heady feeling, up and down the barricades, that the past was about to give way to the strong and good thing that was the future.

Here, though, is an unwelcome fact about kings: they all dream of having the chance to order their armies to push the people back down when they rise up. They just do. It's a big part of why they became kings in the first place.

Another unwelcome fact is that even the most ineffectual of kings cannot be stymied for long by the nondelivery of a single message.

The messenger was on nighttime cooking duty behind the barricade when he heard the first gunshots. He let fall the ladle with which he'd been about to dish out the sweet potato soup he'd helped make. It was salty and good. He had looked forward to being complimented on it.

But now the darkness was shredded by a thousand flames from the thousand muzzles of a thousand soldiers' guns, and the messenger leapt along the top of the barricade past the cowering, bleeding forms of the unarmed protesters, past their curses and prayers and cries of "Murder!" and "Shame!" and somehow past the extremely large number of bullets burying themselves in the stuff the barricade was made of, and then here she was, the messenger's lover, slumped at the center of the barricade, blood pouring from a bullet hole in her neck, and—

"You've come," she said as the messenger cradled her broken form in his arms. Then she died.

The messenger held his former lover and sobbed. His whole body shook, and his whole voice moaned a moan that was, maybe, the song of his life.

He stood up, waved his arms, and shouted, "Kill me! I was the king's messenger. Now I am nothing!"

"Get down!" hissed a protester cringing to the messenger's left.

Shots continued to ring out.

"I was the king's messenger!" the messenger shouted again.

"Hold your fire!" came a voice out of the dark.

The guns ceased their death-throwing then, and there was no sound except the screams of the wounded.

"King's messenger," said the voice that had ordered the cease-fire.

"Kill me," said the messenger.

The voice said something the messenger could not hear. Three soldiers came like ghosts out of the night, clambered up the barricade, seized the messenger by the arm, and hauled him down to the street, away from the body of his beloved.

They took him through the ranks of the killers to where the captain sat at a table drinking espresso.

"Care for a cup?" said the captain.

All around him, the messenger heard the click and snap of guns being reloaded.

"You're safe here," the captain said. "The king will see you tomorrow. But first, an espresso, if you like."

Even now that he had lost his one reason to live, the messenger did not have it in him to refuse a twice-offered espresso.

A cup was handed to him. He drank the espresso fast. It was thick and rich and increasingly bitter toward the bottom.

The captain lit a cigarette and waved it toward the barricade. "Are there any others up there?"

The messenger set his espresso cup down on the table. There was blood on the cup, the blood of the woman he had loved.

"Are there any other infiltrators?" the captain said.

"Infiltrators?" the messenger said. He was thinking that he would have taken his lover to the coast for a holiday once the political impasse had been resolved. He would have brought a map of the stars, and the two of them would have huddled together on the beach, drinking coffee and ascribing meaning to the patterns they saw in the night sky.

The captain scowled. He snuffed his cigarette out against the saucer on which his empty espresso cup sat. Then he turned to the soldiers who had escorted the messenger from the barricade and said, "Take him to the palace."

As they led him away, the messenger heard the captain give the order to resume fire. When the guns boomed again, the messenger doubled over and pressed his face into his bloody hands.

One of the soldiers escorting him bent down and put a hand on the messenger's arm.

"It's a nasty business," the soldier said.

Later, at the palace, the messenger was allowed to bathe and was then shown to a room with a bed in it and a lock on the outside of the door. He slept fitfully, waking up repeatedly to escape a recurring dream in which a doctor kept forcing handfuls of dirt into his mouth.

Morning came. There was a tray of vaguely Greek-seeming food next to the bed. The messenger did not eat but did drink a glass of water.

Before long a guard came and led the messenger down a number of hallways until they came to the king's war room, a dismal basement chamber that the old, good king had never needed to use. The guard went out and closed the door, leaving the messenger alone with the new, terrible king, who folded his hands over his small paunch and said, "Welcome back."

The messenger had been away only eight days, but it could have been eight years, the king was so different. Sitting on his leather-upholstered war-room throne, the king seemed at ease, sure of himself. He was a tyrant now, not just a king. The change suited him. He still had oafish looks and a blocky head, but he seemed to have accepted these things about himself. I am what I am, his bearing proclaimed.

And the messenger—what was he? A grieving lover, a disloyal employee, and a man who had never been so profoundly alone—yes—but what else?

"Espresso?" said the king.

"No," said the messenger. He would not break bread—or coffee beans—with his lover's killer.

"Are you sure?" said the king, smiling maliciously. "I commissioned a new blend called State of Emergency."

The messenger remembered his own state of emergency, which included the very real possibility that his head would be parted from the rest of his body at dawn the next day. This could be his final espresso.

"All right," he said.

The king got up and opened the door and yelled, "Two espressos!" Then he sat down again. There was nowhere for the messenger to sit. He stood looking at the stone floor. How cold the dead must be, he thought.

"We are very grateful to you," said the king. "Taking it upon yourself to infiltrate the ranks of the enemy. A pleasant surprise. You were never one to take the initiative."

The messenger studied the blood-encrusted toes of his own boots.

"Still," said the king, "a king cannot afford to have his servants running around acting on whatever fool notion they take into their little, detachable heads. And you were not a very good spy anyway. You forgot the part about reporting your findings to us."

There came a knock on the war-room door. A sullen-looking servant girl brought the espressos in on a tray. She was a future oil baron, but she did not know that yet. She set the tray down on a table next to the king's throne and left the room.

Unlike the old king, who hadn't stood on ceremony, the new king stood on the idea that no one else could touch his or her espresso until he had finished his. Normally the messenger would have resented having to wait, but today he was more focused on thoughts such as *Am I about to die?* and *I wonder if the king can see that my hands are trembling.*

"I see that your hands are trembling," said the king when he was done with his espresso, "like the hands of a man who is afraid to die. Or perhaps they are trembling because they are so eager to sign this loyalty oath."

The king lifted a piece of paper off the table and held it out to the messenger.

"Sire," said the messenger, "may I drink my espresso first?"

The king nodded.

The messenger blew on his espresso to cool it. He was loath to sign the oath. For one thing, the king was now a tyrant; for another, he had in effect murdered the messenger's one chance at happiness. This was an outrage, the messenger felt, against his own long and nearly unblemished record of perhaps excessively devoted service to the king and his predecessor.

The messenger sipped his espresso.

"God above," he said. "This is first-rate espresso."

The king beamed. "Can you guess which varieties make up the blend?"

The messenger slurped the espresso forcefully, so that it reached all the important taste buds. "Kenya," he said.

"That's one!" cried the king.

The messenger slurped again. "Sumatra?"

"Maybe!" cried the king.

"Maybe?" said the messenger.

"Sign the oath," said the king.

The proper thing to do, the messenger knew, was to refuse to sign and then to follow his lover into the great unknown. That way lay not only higher duty but also, perhaps, glory. The monarchy wouldn't last forever, not in the new king's hands. Today's justly slain rabble-rousers would, tomorrow, be yesterday's martyred heroes. The messenger could be one of them.

Still, voluntarily to give up one's life was, at the time during which this story takes place, a thing more easily contemplated than done.

"Unthinkable," said the messenger.

"Unthinkable that you should sign?" said the king.

"Unthinkable that I should fail to sign," said the messenger.

As he scrawled his name at the bottom of the loyalty oath, the messenger felt almost as though his recently murdered lover were at his side, telling him she didn't love him anymore.

In fact, however, at that moment what was left of her lay motionless and uncomplaining on the barricade as a fly landed on her left eyeball and began cleaning its forelegs.

"So, then," said the messenger. "Is it Sumatra?"

"No," said the king.

And yet Sumatra was not out of the picture entirely. In fact, it was soon in the center of the picture. For the king, unhappy that the messenger had not only joined the resistance but also failed to deliver his message to the captain, fired the messenger as a messenger but then appointed him ambassador to Sumatra.

"But," said the messenger.

"No 'buts,'" said the king. "Your ship sets sail in one hour."

But there was a "but"—a big one. For although the messenger (he still felt like a messenger on the inside even though he was now an ambassador) was on the ship when it set sail, he was also on it five days later when it foundered, as though eagerly, on a shoal that should have been easy to avoid. Everyone aboard died except the messenger, who swam to shore, dried himself off, and began a new life as a shipwrecked older man whose knowledge of the fertile but apparently uninhabited coastal region in which he now found himself was limited to an awareness of its not being Sumatra.

Weeks passed. The messenger made himself strong by eating the bulbous fruits of the strange land. He scanned the horizon by day and the sky by night, hoping either to be rescued or to gain some insight into the human condition. It was nice not to have to hurry from place to place anymore, but then again it was crushingly lousy to be expected nowhere but Sumatra. The messenger wondered whether anyone back home missed him, whether anyone but his creditors would be sad to hear of his nonarrival—assuming the Sumatrans even bothered to fill out the paperwork by which nonarrivals were reported. They were busy growing coffee, after all.

At the thought of coffee, a substance that might never again grace his palate, the messenger began to cry. He cried for a long time, sitting under the fruit tree he had taken to sitting under. He cried for coffee, cried for his dead lover, cried for the happy childhood he dimly remembered. His father had been dead thirty years, and he could no longer exactly picture the old man's face. He couldn't quite call up the face of his own recently deceased lover, either. Sometimes in the morning, when he was just emerging from sleep, the messenger could feel the woman's wispy hair on his fingertips. He had loved how fine it was, had loved the impression it gave of only just barely being subject to gravity. She'd have given anything, she'd told him, for a thicker, bolder head of hair. But when he'd said her hair was beautiful just the way it was, she'd been pleased.

Now she was dead. Had he really even known her? In all his days, was there anyone he had really known? Did he know himself?

The messenger cried himself to sleep that night. He dreamed of artillery and woke to a thunderstorm, the first since he'd crawled ashore. After the storm passed, he lay shivering and wet in the dark. If he didn't do something soon, he understood, he would die alone there on the rocky shore of nowhere.

At dawn, the messenger took off his shirt and tied it into the shape of a sort of bag. He filled it with as many of the bulbous fruits as it would hold. (Hence: "filled.") Then he began walking north, away from the sea.

As he walked, the messenger thought about what it meant to be a messenger. It meant helping people communicate with one another, he supposed. But was that really true? He shooed a fat, brown fly from his arm. What if a messenger actually served as a buffer between people, causing them to lose the art of communicating face to face and thereby speeding the decline of civilization?

But no, he thought, people didn't have time to go running all over the place trying to track down whoever it was they wanted to talk to at that particular moment. And even if they did have that kind of time, they wouldn't spend it that way, because then they wouldn't be at home when other people came looking for them. Messengers were necessary, the messenger concluded.

He stopped to eat a bulbous fruit. He was several miles inland now. The land here appeared less fertile, but there were nice rock formations. It was very quiet, the sound of the sea having fallen away some time ago.

The messenger walked for three days and three nights, stopping only to sleep, to eat, to drink, to relieve himself, to rest, to observe the activities of the local ants, and to fall into various reveries. An idea was taking root in what remained of his mind. He had little enough time left on earth, he knew, for he was an old man. Even if he survived this trek from wherever he'd been to wherever he was going, the best he could hope for was a dignified twilight before the endless night that would blot him out completely.

The idea that was taking root was this: Why should an excellent messenger like him be stuck always working for someone else? Why shouldn't he work for himself, delivering whatever messages he deemed appropriate? Indeed, why shouldn't he deliver messages to the community at large instead of to one person at a time? People needed to hear the same things, mostly—why not be efficient about it?

It was this idea that kept the messenger trudging along despite the increasingly bleak landscape. He hoped one day to find a community in which to try out his new idea.

He was in luck. On the fourth day he came over a rise and descried, there in the distance, a city.

"What is this place?" he asked the first person he saw.

"Zurich," said the person, who was a boy on a bicycle.

"No, it's not," said the messenger. He had been to Zurich. This was not Zurich.

"You're thinking of the other Zurich," said the boy. "This is not that Zurich. This is our Zurich."

The messenger looked at Our Zurich. It seemed as good a city as any in which to try out a new idea.

It was.

The messenger rented a furnished flat in a neighborhood he didn't dislike. He was especially pleased about an old rocking chair that sat in a corner of the bedroom. He would drink coffee in that chair, if coffee could be had in Our Zurich.

Next the messenger bought a bicycle, a small billboard, and a set of wheels. He affixed the wheels to the billboard and the billboard to the back of the bike. His plan was to ride around Our Zurich bringing important messages to the people.

But what did the people need to hear?

The messenger thought about it. Then he wrote on the billboard: *Are you misspending your life?*

He pulled that question from one end of the city to the other.

The people were electrified. A number of them, seeing the sign, fell sobbing to their knees. Others became angry, but not so angry that they were going to hurl abuse at an eccentric old man—even if he was an outlander.

The next day, the messenger asked the people, *Well, then, what about love?*

Reaction to this sign was more muted, although the message did attract a few hecklers. "Lighten up!" they shouted, and "A joke! Tell us a joke!"

On the third day the messenger did tell a joke. On one side of the billboard he wrote, *Why do baby ducklings walk so softly?*

and on the other side, *Because they can't walk, hardly.* This had been his great-grandfather's favorite joke. It was the only joke the messenger knew. It was well received by the people of Our Zurich, if only because they were relieved to read a message that didn't seem like an accusation.

Day after day the messenger made his rounds with his bill-board-on-wheels, and night after night he sat drinking coffee in his rocking chair. Wherever he rode his bike, people waved and blew kisses to him. He didn't let all the attention go to his head, though. He was just happy to be there—happy to have survived a massacre, a shipwreck, and a solo wilderness trek through uncharted territory. Also, he was burning, like wood, with the knowledge that he had not yet delivered his greatest message. But he did not know what that message would be.

He looked for it in the faces of the people of Our Zurich. He looked for it in the way the sunlight moved across the built environment over the course of the day. He even looked for it in the familiar chambers of his own rapidly aging heart. He looked harder than he'd ever looked for anything. But the message did not show itself.

He became desperate. What had begun in, or near, whimsy was now what he had been put on earth to do, he thought. Why else would he have been spared when so many around him had perished? He had been given a second chance, a chance to say what most needed saying. He must not fail.

But it is hard to succeed when your health is declining.

The messenger's health was declining. He was getting too much fresh air and exercise, not enough food or drink, and no sex. Also, he was old.

Nevertheless the messenger continued hauling his burden through the streets of the city. Some of his messages were uninspired: *We're always approaching another fin de siècle* was not his best work. Neither was *What are YOU looking at?* But mostly he tried to be useful, exhorting the people of Our Zurich to floss, to love one another, to keep it real.

He told no one about his obsession with finding the one great message of his life.

One day the messenger's health went from bad to much worse. His heart weakened, his legs gave out, and a permanent headache set in. He managed to drag himself home to his apartment and, once there, to bed. He was tired, tired from the outside of his skin to the marrow of his most central bones. Death was nigh, he knew.

He clung to life, however. A neighbor, a bitter, childless man in his middle years, brought him tea and biscuits every morning and foul-tasting medicines every afternoon. The neighbor even did what was necessary with respect to the messenger's bedpan. He did not talk with the messenger, however. He was a good man but a limited one.

The messenger, too, had been a limited man. This was the central subject of his deathbed ruminations. I have failed, he thought. The Maker made me a messenger, and I have failed to deliver the great message of my life. I do not even know what that message is. I had many years to figure it out, but until the last weeks of my life I didn't even try. I devoted the great part of my energies to shoring up an archaic and unjust political system, all so that I might obtain a piece of paper saying that the building in which I intended to grow old and die was mine. I have been wrong about everything. I have not even managed to fail spectacularly—I have failed in a way that no one will notice. Therefore even my failure will be stripped of its significance the moment I am gone.

Such were the thoughts with which the messenger tortured himself whenever he was awake. When asleep, he dreamed of the great love of his life and of the pageantry that had drawn him into the king's service as a young man. All was love and sex and trumpets in the messenger's feverish dreams.

He died on a Wednesday. But before that happened, this happened:

He woke, clearheaded and calm. It was dark outside, but the lamp by the bed cast a soft light. With some effort, the messenger raised his head and supported it with a pillow. His eye wandered to the old rocking chair in the corner. He had sat in it many times but had never really looked at it. What struck him now was the care with which it had been shaped. The armrests were long and lean, and they curved gently upward toward their front ends, which were rounded to provide a comfortable grip for the sitter's hands. The wood there was worn smooth from long use—it waxed golden in the lamplight. How many pairs of hands had caressed this wood that had been so painstakingly fashioned for them? How many other souls had preceded the messenger in the use of this unlikely thing, this chair? The world was haunted, the messenger felt, haunted not by death but by life. Life thrummed in all things. It thrummed even in the dying messenger. It was everywhere, always, nearer than words, nearer than breath. To attempt to say anything about it was already to have forgotten what it was. Open your mouth to speak and you were already wrong.

Acknowledgments

Thanks to the editors of the publications in which the following stories first appeared:

The Anthology of New England Writers: "Men";
Backwards City Review: "Against Specificity";
Dogzplot: "I'm Sorry I Lost the Scrap of Paper on Which You Outlined Your Plans for the Future" and "My Memoir";
Ecotone: "New Animal";
Fifty-two Stories: "Against Specificity";
The Journal: "The Death of John O'Brien," "Narrative of the Life of Jacob Livesey," and "Wolves";
Ohio Writer: "Author Sentenced for Life";
Other Rooms: "My Foot Is on Fire";
Salt Hill: "What I Did on My Summer Vacation";
Sou'wester: "The Cave," "The Era of Not Quite," and "The Man Who Was Cast into the Void";
Tin House Flash Fridays: "Life on the Moon."

The Kierkegaard quotations in "New Animal" are taken from the 1849 essay "The Sickness Unto Death: A Christian Psychological Exposition for Upbuilding and Awakening," in *The Essential Kierkegaard*, edited by Howard V. Hong and Edna H. Hong (Princeton University Press, 2000), page 352.

For teaching me more than I will ever know about writing, I thank Blake Maher, Bruce Machart, Lee K. Abbott, Erin McGraw, and, most of all, my MFA thesis director, Michelle Herman. For their friendship and literary co-conspiratorship, I thank Kyle Minor, Bart Skarzynski, Sean Flanigan, Maureen Traverse, and Tom Jundt. Thanks to Ohio State University and the Sewanee Writers' Conference for their money and other things. Here's to Grub Street Writers, Sackett Street Writers, and the Greenpoint Writers Group. I am deeply indebted to Peter Conners and the rest of the team at BOA, as well as to Anne Borchardt and Samantha Shea at Georges Borchardt, Inc. To my mother and father I owe everything. To my brothers I owe a lot. To the people I'm neglecting to mention I owe an apology. Above all, for her love, support, and patience—and for being my first and best reader—thanks to Michelle Burke.

About the Author

Douglas Watson holds an MFA in creative writing from Ohio State University. His fiction has appeared in *Fifty-two Stories, Tin House Flash Fridays, Salt Hill, Sou'wester, The Journal, Ecotone,* and other publications. His story "Life on the Moon" was chosen by Dan Chaon and *Wigleaf* in 2012 as one of the year's top fifty very short fictions. He lives in Brooklyn and works as a copyeditor for *Time* magazine. *The Era of Not Quite* is his first book.

BOA Editions, Ltd., American Reader Series

Colophon

The Era of Not Quite, stories by Douglas Watson, is set in Monotype Dante. First created in metal type in the mid-1950s and digitalized in the 1990s, it is the result of a collaboration between Giovanni Mardersteig—a printer, book designer, and typeface artist renowned for the work he produced at Officina Bodoni and Stamperia Valdònega in Italy—and Charles Malin, one of the great punch-cutters of the twentieth century.

The publication of this book is made possible, in part, by the special support of the following individuals:

Anonymous x 2
Peter & Karen Conners
Anne Germanacos
Michael Hall
Robert & Willy Hursh
X. J. & Dorothy M. Kennedy
Jack & Gail Langerak
Boo Poulin
Steven O. Russell & Phyllis Rifkin-Russell
Sue S. Stewart, *in memory of Stephen L. Raymond*
Gerald Vorrasi

Printed in the USA
CPSIA information can be obtained
at www.ICGtesting.com
JSHW082351140824
68134JS00020B/2006